This picture of my father, Fritz Wolf, was taken in May of 1936 when he was just 10 years old. The Nuremberg Laws had been passed in his hometown of Nuremberg, Germany 6 months prior to this changing his life forever. Except for a quick snapshot his mother took as she left him in France hoping to shield him from the Nazis, this is the last picture we have until 1947. The Nazis stole the years between these pictures of him, but they could not steal his hope and tenacity.

This book is dedicated to my
amazing family and to my
father whose story impacts all
of us.

This Too Shall Pass

Kathleen Wolf Peppin

Prologue

It was a quiet, still night on a farm nestled in the
countryside of Southern France on an April night in 1943.
Suddenly, there were blaring lights, screeching tires, and
men shouting. The scene turned instantly from serene and
pastoral to chaotic and frightening. Since everything
happened at such a rapid pace, there was no time to run to
the fields to hide as the residents had done on previous
occasions. Nazi soldiers holding guns and restraining
attack dogs stormed the house and the buildings
surrounding it. Someone had tipped them off that the
property owners, a kind farmer and his wife, had been ·
hiding Jews. The soldiers found two terrified boys in the
loft of the barn. Both were arrested and taken in darkness
to prison. One was 16-year-old Fritz Wolf, my father.
The other was his 15-year-old cousin, Ernst. They were

eventually deported to separate concentration camps where each thought the other had perished. Miraculously fifty years later, Ernst found my father and they were reunited. On that day I finally heard the story of the horrors my father endured during the Holocaust from his own lips.

This one day held many surprises and twists and turns. I was forty-one years old and had given up entirely on knowing what had happened during those dark years of my father's life. I know God orchestrated it so I would be in Salt Lake City visiting my widowed father on the exact day I needed to be there. I still, to this day, marvel at what happened and that I was with him to experience his miracle and have one of my own.

My favorite memories of visiting my widowed father from out of state were the early mornings as we sipped coffee and talked uninterrupted by the day's coming distractions. That morning I looked forward especially to the very precious time we would have. But, as we were enjoying our coffee, we were interrupted by the shrill and intrusive ringing of the phone in the kitchen. It is strange the things we remember but my dad still had a rotary phone connected to the wall. He swore cell phones had bad reception and he couldn't hear people on them. There was no changing his mind on things like that; he would dig his heels in and become quite stubborn. He kept the phone turned to its highest volume, so he could hear it anywhere in the house. If we were close, the ringing was a high, loud unpleasant sound. Sometimes I would jump when it rang, and I certainly did this time because it caught me off guard. That infuriating ringing was interrupting our quiet interlude, so I resented it. Who would call this early in the morning?

My father jumped from his chair and ran to answer the phone. As soon as he answered he heard a click because the caller had hung up. The scene became bizarre. Over and over again the phone would ring, and the caller would hang up. Dad would walk back to the living room and just as he sat down, the phone would ring again. He couldn't be convinced to unplug the phone and of course we couldn't ignore that irritating ring so on and on it went.

Finally, the caller stayed on the line. Dad sank to his chair: "My God! My God!" he repeated over and over. I frantically flew into the kitchen to find out what was wrong. He signaled with hand that everything was okay and brushed me away. He kept saying, "I cannot believe this! You have come back from the dead." The mysterious caller was his cousin Ernst, who he had long believed to be dead, calling from the airport. At first, I had no idea who on earth Ernst was because of the secrecy that had always surrounded my father's life in Germany. His name had never been mentioned. All at once a remarkable story was pouring from my father. After all the years of silence, he was sharing his story with me. I stood transfixed and dumbfounded by what I was hearing. In my mind I had imagined my father's story many times trying piece together what might have happened. What he was telling me was more amazing than any story I could have ever imagined. It was believed that Ernst had perished at Auschwitz with his entire family. Now we were finding out that he alone survived and had found my father almost fifty years to the day after they had been arrested together.

But it was just beginning. I was about to find out many astonishing things. My father had to explain who Ernst was and how they were arrested together as we eagerly waited for Ernst to arrive. I could barely take it all in and felt like a child running to keep up. My dad was hidden in a barn? Arrested and thrown in jail? There was no time to ask questions or even process what I was hearing. He had to catch me up fast. Ernst was on his way.

Ernst had been living in Chicago and Denver for many years. He finally put some puzzle pieces together and traced the little family that had survived. He somehow found my father's address and phone number. Ernst had then flown to Salt Lake and was planning to surprise his long-lost cousin, but the emotion of it all had gotten the best of him. He was too overcome to speak which is why he kept hanging up. He finally found the courage to stay on the line and choke out who he was. Both men were left in tears. I did not yet know the entire story but as a grown woman I could surely understand the emotions these two men shared, together at last after fifty years of separation.

Their reunion brought indescribable joy but also much pain. They kept saying, "This is like seeing a ghost." I sat in the very same room where just an hour before my dad and I had been having a normal, everyday conversation. Now I became invisible and that was just fine with me. I was able to witness a true-life miracle of two men who were lost in time and seemed to forget I was there.

At first all the two men could do was cry and hug and marvel that they were reunited. They were transported back to Germany in their minds. The clock had turned back fifty years. "I can't believe it!" was repeated over and over again. Time seemed to stand still. Finally, two stories of incredible pain poured out. I was afraid to move, even, for fear the spell might be broken but I doubt my presence or lack thereof would have made a difference to those two men.

Fritz and Ernst had been arrested by the Nazis on a frightening day in April of 1943. They were just 16 and 15, two terrified teenagers hidden in the loft of a barn by a kind farmer in southern France. Ernst was deported to Auschwitz and Fritz was taken to Nuremberg, his hometown, where he was tried as a member of the French Resistance. He was then sentenced to a concentration camp in France. He suffered unspeakable atrocities in the concentration camp but miraculously escaped and lived through the Allied bombing of Nuremberg, narrowly escaping death again. All this happened before he saw his nineteenth birthday.

That day I witnessed the power of God in a life and learned what forgiveness really means. There was an enormous contrast between the two men even though they had shared so many experiences. As they talked Ernst became more and more agitated and distraught. By contrast, my father had a serene composure about him. Ernst finally asked, "How can you talk about the Nazis and remain so untroubled?" My father's reply visibly shocked Ernst. "I chose to forgive the Nazis." That one simple sentence was profound. Ernst replied angrily, "How could you? What they did was unforgivable. I will never forgive them!" My father looked at Ernst with compassion because he knew well the hell Ernst was living. He had lived that same hell for years. In a loving yet firm way he shared how forgiving the Nazis had freed him. Ernst refused to listen and became even angrier. I realized the high cost of unforgiveness that day. It created its own prison sentence. My father not only talked the talk, he walked the walk. His life reflected God's love and forgiveness and with that profound peace. It was a lesson I will never forget. The Nazis still held Ernst prisoner. My father was free.

I am writing this story for my family. I want future generations never to forget the Holocaust and the lessons learned from it. I also want to tell the story of a great man most of them will never know. But his story gives me the opportunity also to share God's love, mercy, and power and the circumstances we could all find ourselves in if we remain apathetic in life. I have written this to the best of my knowledge and ability with the facts that I have. There are many holes in this story, things I will never know. I sometimes wish I could go back in time and ask my father the questions that now haunt me. Until I wrote his story, I didn't even think of them. I also wish I could go back and record what he told me. I was caught off guard every time he talked about Germany since that fateful day with Ernst and I was never prepared to take notes. He never told his sister or mother or father what happened to him in the camp. Only his beloved wife, Dorothy, heard his entire story. His sister took her story to the grave. She just could never talk about it. This is a painful yet beautiful story. I can still see the anguish in my father's eyes whenever he talked about the Nazis and I realize that I probably still wouldn't ask him any more questions. I would not want to cause him to relive that pain one more time. I struggled for a long time with whether I should even write this. I finally realized that it was a story that needed to be told. Perhaps that is why God allowed me to hear it.

My father's story began in Nuremberg, Germany where Arnold Wolf, a Jew, met Anna Fischer, a Lutheran, and they fell in love......

Chapter One

"Believe me our misery will increase."

Adolf Hitler 1923

In the year my grandparents, Arnold and Anna, met and fell in love, little could they have imagined that their beloved homeland was on the brink of her darkest hour. Nor could they know how the sudden rise of a maniacal dictator would shatter their seemingly idyllic lives. And, of course, they did not know that nearly one hundred years later, their granddaughter would seek to uncover a story that crossed the boundaries of several countries, a century, and an ocean.

They lived in the enchanting medieval city of Nuremberg considered "The Jewel of Bavaria," a province in Germany. The beautiful city center, surrounded by a medieval wall, was distinguished by its striking architecture of ancient red-roofed half-timbered buildings and ornate gothic churches. The centerpiece of the town was the elegantly gilded Beautiful Fountain rising from an octagonal basin to a church-like spire in the sky and containing 40 colorful images representing the Holy Roman Empire. In the Haufmart, or town square, merchants set up booths of fresh foods and flowers with vibrant displays of colors and smells. Picturesque bridges crossed the Pegnitz River running through town. In December of each year Nuremberg hosted the grandest Christmas market in all of Europe visited by people from all over the world. On a hill overlooking the city sat the Imperial Castle, large and imposing; its original stone wall extended from the castle to surround and protect the city. The castle had been an inspiring symbol of Nuremberg's prominence since the middle ages. Representing the power and importance of the German nation, it brought a sense of strength and pride to the people. Built in 1050 the castle eventually became the official meeting place of the Holy Roman Empire's parliaments and courts marking it as a stronghold of the empire. All German kings and emperors stayed there. By 1219, Nuremberg was given an Imperial title and became the unofficial capital of the Holy Roman Empire. Because of its enviable status, the city prospered as one of the most important towns in all of Germany. By the late middle ages, it was acknowledged as the most distinguished, best located city of the realm. For 500 years Nuremberg represented the power and importance of the Holy Roman Empire and was connected with the most significant developments in German history.

Hitler would one day call Nuremberg the "Most German of German cities" and name that 500 years of Germany's imperial reign, "The First Reich." Soon, thousands upon thousands of Nazi soldiers would march through the same streets Arnold and Anna strolled, holding hands and dreaming of a bright future. Massive Nuremberg rallies would be held yearly, and Jews would be marched through the city center on their way to concentration camps while people looked the other way as they went about their daily business. This charming city, famous for gingerbread and sausages, would soon be covered in Swastika Flags and filled with anti-Jewish propaganda. No building would be spared the posters filled with grotesque pictures showing Jews as beasts to be feared. By the end of World War II as Nuremberg lay in ruins, she would no longer be called the Jewel of

Bavaria, but would be forever known as The Birthplace of the Nazis, a black stain that would always haunt her. For such a hideous evil to be born in a place of beauty would be impossible to comprehend. As the Irish poet, W. B. Yeats had written in 1916, "All changed, changed utterly. A terrible beauty is born." How could anyone have conceived that Germany would lose her very soul? Certainly not Arnold and Anna who, like all young lovers, must have been filled with hope, not foreboding.

In 1920 when Anna Fischer and Arnold Wolf met, Germany was headed for an economic collapse. Living in a country devastated by a humiliating defeat in WWI the Germans were further crippled when forced to sign the Treaty of Versailles on June 28, 1919. The treaty was a deadly blow to the already deflated German people and forced Germany to accept sole responsibility for causing the war, to disarm, to make territorial concessions, and pay reparations in an amount equivalent to 3.5 billion dollars. Due to Versailles, Germany was forced to pay incredibly large sums of money to France and Great Britain which generated great hatred for France and England. The German people also blamed their government for undermining Germany's efforts in the final stages of the war and signing the hated treaty. To recover from the war, the government initiated social programs to create jobs for the German people. Social spending began rising at an unsustainable rate. Faced with reparation payments they could not afford and out of control government spending, Germany began printing exaggerated amounts of money which created almost unimaginable inflation. Unlike France which imposed their first ever income tax to pay for the war, Germany chose to fund its war efforts entirely by borrowing money which also helped to throw the country into hyperinflation. German currency became worthless. The people were frightened and desperate for relief. They distrusted their government and were ready to find blame for the mess they were in.

This seemed the perfect time for Adolph Hitler, a young, charismatic new leader, to emerge on the political scene. His National Socialist Party was officially formed on April 1, 1920. An agitator and eloquent speaker, Hitler railed against the Versailles Treaty stating he would make it invalid. He also blamed the Jews for the mess Germany was in. He promised to unify the German people and restore them to their former glory. the anti-Semitic points of his program were publicly proclaimed and put in writing.

Jews would be denied citizenship in Germany and excluded from working in the press. It is the world's misfortune that these dire warnings were ignored.

The devastation of WW1 had a tremendous impact on Arnold and Anna. Anna lived through meager rations, cold, and hunger. Arnold soldiered in trenches literally described as a hell on earth. Germany opened the war on the Western Front when they invaded France on August 3, 1914. The German people assumed this would be a swift and sure victory. Instead the war lasted four and a half long, grueling years. Germany was ill prepared to fight a lengthy war. Civilians suffered greatly especially during the long cold winters. The human cost of the war was startling. Of the three million German soldiers who fought in the war, more than two million perished in the conflict. Even though German soil was not invaded, more than 750,000 civilians died from cold and starvation. Few cultures can sustain losses like those.

As a result, World War 1 profoundly altered the lives of all German people. Their world was changed forever. Perhaps that is what influenced Arnold and Anna to leave their conservative roots and the religion of their childhoods. Many younger Germans were disillusioned with their government at this point and restless. They were rejecting childhood religious beliefs in favor of liberal teachings. Arnold and Anna belonged to a group of young people in Nuremberg who were considered liberal and progressive. These young people were patriotic, enthusiastic, and ready to change the course of German politics.

Anna Fischer had just turned eighteen when the war started. She had been born in Nuremberg on May 15, 1896, one of six children of Georg, a factory worker, and Margarete, a homemaker. Georg worked long, hard days in the factory to support his large family. Working conditions were brutal in the factories; they were dirty, dark, and dusty and men worked six days a week sometimes for sixteen hours a day. Even though they were poor, the Fischer children were loved and well cared for. The household was lively and Anna, the fun-loving extrovert of the family, thrived in this environment. The Lutheran church was an important component of the Fischer family's life. Anna loved the moving ceremonies and hauntingly beautiful music the Lutherans did so well. Even when she renounced religion and called herself an agnostic, she could not give up the holiday celebrations of her childhood church. She would later take her children to Christmas and Easter services with her family. After the Holocaust she completely turned her back on religion and never darkened the door of a church again.

Holidays, especially Christmas, were celebrated with great enthusiasm by the Fischer family. Even though they had little money, Margarete made Christmas special in little ways for her family. They had gifts and treats and an extended large family to celebrate with. Christmas would always be special to Anna.

Everything changed with the outbreak of the war. With the men at war, ordinary housewives were forced to work in the factories to support their families. Anna had to disrupt her education and go to work to help support the family. Fortunately, she had typing skills and was able to work as a secretary. Most women had to work long, strenuous days in hot, dirty factories. Food was scarce during those years and life was harsh. The most nutritious food was used for the soldiers. Civilians became creative with what they had. Potatoes became the main staple of the people. The winter of 1916-1917 was particularly severe and became known as the "Turnip Winter." An early frost killed the potatoes, but turnips survived. This hardly edible vegetable became the mainstay of the people. Everyone in Germany was perpetually hungry that winter and many thousands starved to death. By the time the war ended, Anna was 22 and still working as a secretary. She left her conservative roots and denounced formal religion.

Arnold was born to Abraham and Marie Wolf in Bad Durkheim Germany in 1885. His father was a successful wine merchant and the family lived comfortably above his shop. Two years later Greta would join the family. Arnold was raised in an Orthodox Jewish home with strict adherence to Jewish laws and practices. Attending Synagogue was central to the Wolf family's lives. Jewish holidays were kept sacred with Abraham leading the family in prayers and candle lighting and special readings. Today in Israel a book of prayers, signed and dated by Abraham in 1887, is read by his great grandson, Jacques, on Rosh Hashanah every year to his children and grandchildren. Greta kept the faith of her childhood and it has been passed down to her children, grandchildren, and great grandchildren. These rituals were moving and meaningful to Arnold and unlike Anna, he returned to the faith of his childhood after the Holocaust.

Arnold's life, unlike Anna's, was structured and disciplined. Abraham sadly died young at only 50 years of age and Arnold, just a teenager, was forced to become the man of the family. It was a devastating loss. Marie ran the family business by herself while raising two children. She was a shrewd businesswoman and the business prospered. As a mother, Marie was strict and uncompromising. Arnold attended the very best schools and received a first-rate education. Perhaps due to the untimely death of his father when he was so young, Arnold had an unusually strong bond with his mother. Like both of his parents, he had a flair for business and was on the path to a successful career.

Arnold was 29 when Germany entered the war and he was conscripted into the army. It was a horrendous war for the soldiers. Most men fought in dark, wet, trenches with little food or supplies. Death was all around them. Much has been written about the horrors of the front-line trenches during WWI. The soldiers returned to Germany profoundly changed by the experience; they who had fought so hard, became bitter when Germany admitted defeat and signed the dreaded Treaty of Versailles. They felt their government had betrayed and stabbed them in the back. Many soldiers, like Arnold, became pacifists after the war and wanted peace at all costs. Others became militant socialists perpetuating the "stabbed in the back" theory. This militant group contributed significantly to the rise of Adolph Hitler and another world war.

Arnold returned to his job after the war and was transferred to Nuremberg. Like Anna, he had left the faith of his parents and no longer attended synagogue or participated in the Jewish rituals that had been so important to him in her earlier years. By 1920 he was again on his way to a very successful career. Finally, both he and Anna hoped the future would again be bright for Germany. They had been bruised and battered by the horrible war, but they had a new optimism and energy and were eager to make a difference in German politics.

Arnold and Anna met in Nuremberg when Arnold became part of Anna's group of friends. Anna at 23 was a bit stocky with blue eyes and blonde hair cut in a fashionable bob. With her beautiful smile and quick wit, she was the life of the party. She and her friends loved to picnic in the beautiful German countryside as well as play card games and enjoy the vibrant social life of that time. Anna was an intelligent, independent woman. Her circle of friends was liberal and modern in their thinking and they loved to discuss and debate the political scene in Germany. They were patriotic, energetic, and eager to make a difference in their world.

Arnold was a handsome man with dark hair and penetrating brown eyes. He sported a fashionable mustache and was impeccably dressed and groomed. It's easy to see how he caught Anna's eye when he moved to Nuremberg and joined her circle of friends. At 34 he was successful, intelligent, and handsome, a good catch for any woman. There was a problem; he was a confirmed bachelor and a momma's boy.

Arnold and Anna seemed opposites in every way. Spirited and young, Anna embraced life with optimism and passion. Arnold, proper and serious, was eleven years her senior. She was happy and carefree while he was a born worrier and cautious about every decision he made. She loved to be with people and thrived on activity. He was a loner and enjoyed long, quiet walks in the country. He was Jewish and she was Lutheran. He might have been captivated by her sense of humor and outgoing personality. She was probably drawn to Arnold's good looks and intelligence. Despite all these differences they did have some common ground. Both loved to read, especially classics, both loved classical music, and both were passionate about politics. Eventually they fell in love.

Even though Arnold and Anna were involved in German politics, they probably paid very little attention to the small new socialist party that Adolph Hitler established the year they met. At first, the National Socialist Party seemed to be an assortment of misfits. But as the economic crisis deepened, Hitler capitalized on the chaotic conditions and his party started gaining momentum. With Germany at her weakest point, Hitler took the opportunity to begin his rise to power. Hitler used the Jewish people as a scapegoat for all Germany's problems. He was throwing the hungry, desperate people a lifeline.

By 1923 Arnold and Anna had been engaged for several years and were waiting for his mother's approval to marry. Predictably, Marie was dead set against the marriage. Not only was Anna not Jewish, she was the daughter of a factory worker. Marie felt like it was beneath her son to marry her and she wouldn't budge. It was a new position for Arnold to be in since he had always lived to please his mother. Both the women he loved were stubborn and Marie had met her match. Poor, patient Anna waited years for Arnold to defy his mother or for his mother to bless their marriage. Neither Arnold nor Anna thought religion would be an important part of their decision. How could Anna know what marrying a Jew would cost her?

By now, hyperinflation was out of control in Germany. With the shelves on the stores bare and long lines for even a loaf of bread, money meant very little. In 1923 Germany suffered the wildest inflation in history. It took 200 billion marks to buy a loaf of bread. A day's wages for a factory worker was enough only for a loaf of bread and piece of cheese. People brought wheelbarrows and baskets filled with money to stand in the bread lines. Thieves would steal the baskets and wheelbarrows but leave the money untouched. Farmers refused to bring their produce to the cities in return for worthless money and food riots broke out. Unemployment soared. Desperate people began bringing valuable works of art, furniture, and jewelry to trade for food. Even though the government stepped in and ended the hyperinflation quickly, millions of middle-class Germans were financially ruined from the ordeal. They became fertile soil for Hitler's rise to power.

The state of Bavaria had reached a point of crisis. The political scene around them was pure chaos. People were frustrated and demanding change. Bavaria was threatening a revolt from Berlin. The people were ready to establish their own independence from the hated Republic. Adolph Hitler was leading a revolt to overthrow the entire Republic and unite the country. He envisioned himself the ruler of the entire country, not just Bavaria. "Believe me our misery will increase" he shouted. "We will no longer submit to a state which is built on the swindling idea of the majority. We want a dictatorship!" Hitler's popularity was growing in Bavaria. Millions of Germans felt he was the one to lead them on. Even though the Nazi party was growing daily in numbers, it was relatively unknown outside of Bavaria. Nuremberg was in the very heart of the State of Bavaria and Arnold and Anna were caught in the political uncertainty. Hitler raged against the Jews and the Nazi party gained momentum. In all the confusion and unrest Arnold, himself a Jew, could only hope Hitler would fail.

On November 8, 1923, Hitler tried and failed to start a national revolution by overthrowing the Bavarian government. He and his troops stormed a police meeting being held at a beer hall in Munich. Hitler shouted, "The National Revolution has begun!" The coup was thwarted, and Hitler arrested. The Nazi party to all appearances was dead. Arnold, like many Jews, was probably relieved that the absurd idea that a man like Hitler could control Germany.

Arnold

Anna

Nuremberg

Children play with money and woman
burns it during hyperinflation

Hitler in an Early Rally

Chapter 2

"A wonderful ferment was working in Germany. Life seemed more free, more modern, and more exciting than any place I had ever been."

William Shirer 1925

Finally, on June 11, 1924, Anna Fischer became the wife of Arnold Wolf in a small intimate ceremony in Nuremberg. What brought this epic stand-off between Arnold and his mother to an end? The rumor mill ran wild in our family with this one. Did Anna give an ultimatum? Did Maria finally give up? Maybe they did the unthinkable in the 1920's and move in together, or as my aunt said they may have had an indiscretion. Why someone didn't ask her and clear this up while she was alive is a mystery that likely will never be solved.

Arnold was 39 and Anna 28 when they married. His mother did not survive the Holocaust. If she had, she would have known that Arnold's life and those of his children were spared because of his marriage; through history, few wives have so dramatically saved their families from death. Had Arnold married a Jewish girl, he and his family would certainly have perished in the Holocaust.

In that year Germany was beginning to pull out of economic crisis. After years of hunger, deprivation, and defeat, the people were still wary but relieved. With the loss of a long and hard-fought war that practically destroyed an entire generation, the humiliating Treaty of Versailles, and a crippled economy, they were tired, battered and bruised. On February 26 of that year Adolph Hitler was tried and convicted of treason. His sentence was astoundingly mild. Treason normally carried a sentence of life in prison. He was sentenced to five years in prison and would be eligible for parole after serving only six months. He started his imprisonment high above the Lech River in an old fortress where he was treated as an honored guest. He had become a hero in the eyes of many Germans. While in prison he wrote his famous book, *Mein Kampf* (My Struggle) and strategized how his Nazi party could regain power and position in Germany.

As the economic crisis loosened its grip, Arnold and Anna started their married life with a new optimism shared generally by the German people. The young couple purchased a charming row house on Hermstatten Strasse (in English, Hermstatten Street) in an upscale, desirable area of Nuremberg. Hermstatten was a postcard perfect street with houses three stories high graced with red steep-pitched roofs that were the trademark of Nuremberg's distinct architecture. With much excitement and enthusiasm, Arnold and Anna furnished their new home with exquisite, ornate, hand-carved furniture. Anna chose simple, elegant white Rosenthal china to go with her delicate crystal and elegant silver. She had impeccable taste and her home was decorated accordingly. Arnold, with his love of gardening, planted lovely flower and vegetable gardens in the yard. Their street was full of friendly, young successful couples like Arnold and Anna.

Arnold's job required extensive travel and so Anna enjoyed her many friends and activities while he was gone. Her new life with Arnold must have seemed like a page from a story book. With a full-time maid as well as a seamstress and laundress, it was beyond what the daughter of a poor factory worker could have dreamed of.

Anna loved to entertain and throw lavish parties. Ever the fun-loving practical jokester, family lore has it that she would inevitably try to trick her guests. At one party she put paper in the finger sandwiches instead of cheese. People said that you never knew what surprises Anna had up her sleeve. After dinner, guests would gather around the piano to sing lively songs accompanied by Arnold, a gifted pianist. Anna, with her outgoing personality, fit right in with her social neighbors. She was passionate about the game of Bridge and played for hours every day in the neighborhood card clubs. Their social circles became close and tight knit with the adults enjoying dinner parties and card games while their children played together.

Times were good by 1926. It was the era of the roaring 20's in the United States. The economy in Germany was booming. Unemployment was down, retail sales up and salaries had risen. The German people began to enjoy the new prosperity that swept their country. William Shirer, a young reporter from America and author of *Rise and Fall of the Third Reich*, described the social scene in Paris and London as bland in comparison to cities like Berlin and Munich. "A wonderful ferment was working in Germany" he said. "Life seemed more free, more modern, more exciting than in any place I had ever been." In Nuremberg the atmosphere was lively and invigorating as the people relished their new freedom from the old repressive days. The arts had sprung back to life in a city that prided itself in music, literature, and fine art. People had passionate, heated discussions in sidewalk cafes and plush bars all over town. Arnold and Anna enjoyed grand evenings out with their friends taking in the splendid symphonies, operas, and theaters Nuremberg had to offer. Anna dressed in elegant dresses usually accessorized with an elaborate brooch and a stylish hat. Arnold wore custom-tailored suits with his starched shirt collar folded just right above the lapel of his jacket and a broad, silk tie. Later in the evening they joined in the lively discussions at the sidewalk cafes. The energy and optimism of the young people was refreshing, and discussions often lasted until the early morning hours. They probably were no longer discussing Adolph Hitler or the Nazi party anymore. By now most Germans thought Hitler was finished even though he had been released from prison in December of 1924 after serving only nine months of his sentence. After his release the Nazi party and its press were banned, and Hitler was forbidden from speaking in public. How could he possibly ever become a force in politics with such restrictions upon his activities and person?

Hitler had profited by the country's suffering. Now that the nation's outlook was bright, people expected him to fade out of the picture. The minister of Justice declared about him, "The wild beast is checked." But, as we now know in hindsight, they were wrong. Hitler was busy regrouping and reorganizing. He called for a "New Beginning" for the Nazi party. Hitler was confident the good times would not last. He was right in realizing that the strength of the new economy was dependent on loans from other countries, especially American investors. It had to eventually collapse on itself. He had the patience to wait out the good years while he crafted a new strategy for his party. He had a mythical sense that his destiny in life was to build a glorious new Germany.

Anna's happiest news that year was that she was expecting a baby. In the eyes of their relatives and friends they might have seemed too old to be starting a family. Anna would be 30 and Arnold 41 when the baby arrived. Despite that, both were elated since neither thought parenthood was possible for them. On the night of August third after a long and difficult labor, Anna gave birth to a healthy baby boy. A son! They were overjoyed. The greatest blessing for a Jewish father was the birth of a son and Arnold still held that in his heart. They chose the name Fritz Gustav for their new son, Fritz because they liked the name and Gustav to honor Arnold's father. Two years later Gertrude Marianne joined the family. Blessed with a son and a daughter, Arnold and Anna's family was perfect and complete. Anna was a fun, happy mother who adored her children and loved to spoil them. She had grown up in a lively chaotic household and wanted the same for her children, Arnold, on the other hand, had been raised in a quiet orderly household with rigid rules and strict discipline. He was the quieter, stricter parent. With his spirited wife and two children arriving within two years, his quiet disciplined life had been turned upside down.

Fritzlah--Little Fritz as he was affectionately called was to all accounts a handsome baby. As he grew into toddlerhood, he had blond curls and a cherubic face. His mother dressed him in delicate, feminine looking rompers, the style of that day for baby and toddler boys. In a picture of Fritz as a young toddler, one immediately thinks, "What a darling angel". This angelic looking boy had a temper though. The maid many times became fed up with his tantrums and threw cold water on him to quiet him down. But to his mother he could do no wrong. Strong-willed from the start and mischievous, he kept the household on their toes. Fritz was just two years old when his sister Gertrude was born. Luckily for the whole family he adored his sister and took his role of big brother quite seriously. Calm and quiet Gertrude was the exact opposite of her brother although she, too, was a beautiful child with blue eyes and long blond curls. As Fritz grew older Anna dressed him in smart little suits with short pants and shiny black shoes. Always the princess in the family, Gertrude wore frilly dresses with large bows adorning her long blonde hair. Anna would go to a children's shop she loved in town and buy armloads of new clothes for the children. She couldn't resist the little suits for Fritz and lovely dresses for Gertrude. An oft repeated cycle began, Arnold, who Anna considered miserly, would complain that she had spent too much. Anna would promise to return the clothes. Her strategy was to buy five dresses for Gertrude and when Arnold complained, return two of them. Then she could tell him, "Yes, I returned Gertrude's dresses today." Her response might not have been entirely truthful, but neither was it totally disingenuous.

As an adult Fritz reminisced about his early childhood in the most idyllic of terms. It was a magical time in his memory. Arnold and Anna insulated their children from the devastating events surrounding them. Fritz was only three when the great depression swept Germany. He was oblivious in the years to follow of the economic crisis and political unrest of his country. Sadly, the day would come when his loved ones could no longer shelter or protect him.

One of Fritz's earliest childhood memories was of trains. He had an obsession for them as long as he could remember. He loved watching them rumble through town, piercing the air with their whistles. The biggest treat for him as a young boy was to get to go to the train station. He was always begging someone to take him. The very best part of visiting his Oma in Bad Durkheim was that she lived right on the main street of town and he could walk right out of the door and be at that wonderful train station where, if permitted, he would watch the trains all day. He was captivated not only with the trains but also with the activity of the station. For hours he would watch the trains switching tracks and coming and leaving the station. Arnold was not the demonstrative parent Anna was, but he related to his children in his own quiet way. Fritz enjoyed leisurely walks with his father in the evenings and "helping" him in the vegetable garden. Arnold transformed the backyard with fruit trees, berry hedges, and a magnificent vegetable garden. Fritz and Gertrude "helped" their father by picking the delicious fruit and berries and eating them. Both Arnold and Anna were avid readers and imparted a love of books to their children. They had wonderful children's books in their home and the children were read to often. Every summer Fritz vacationed with his family at his aunt's cottage in the beautiful German countryside. Many members of Anna's large family would join them providing Fritz and Gertrude numerous cousins to play with.

Fritz showed unusual intelligence at an early age. His parents felt he was destined for great things and determined to get him in the best schools Germany had to offer. There was no doubt in their minds that someday he would attend a distinguished university and become something great. At age six Fritz was enrolled in an extremely strict and demanding school. Already at this young age he had hours of homework every night. The students were required to dress properly (for Fritz that meant a suit and tie) and the teachers demanded complete obedience. Fritz loved school and thrived on the disciplined environment. He was an excellent student and soaked up information like a sponge. By age 10, he was tested and qualified to attend an advanced school with a rigorous academic schedule. His favorite subjects were math and history. Like his father, Fritz showed a gift for the piano. His parents started him in lessons early and required hours of diligent practice. Because his father had instilled an appreciation of classical music in him, learning to play the beautiful pieces made piano practice a pleasure not a chore. His ambition was to play as well as his father. Card games were Anna's passion. She taught her son simple games until he was old enough to learn the complicated game of Bridge. Eventually he had an equal passion for Beethoven and Bridge, satisfying both parents. In the evenings after dinner Arnold and Anna would engage their children in lively debates. Both father and son possessed enormous stubborn streaks and as Fritz grew older the debates could become heated and last well into the evening.

Perhaps the best part of the day for Fritz and Gertrude was right after school. There were always children in their neighborhood waiting to play with them. Fritz would eagerly change his clothes and run out as fast as he could to play with his friends. Wrestling matches were popular with the boys and Fritz would win almost all of them. He was as talented physically as he was intellectually.

Holidays were Anna's time to shine. She went all out for every holiday and special occasion. Christmas, Easter, New Year's Eve, and birthday celebrations were especially memorable. Even though religion was not practiced in the home, Arnold and Anna must have had an agreement about Christmas. Anna could not give that up. Those holidays held precious memories from her childhood, and she wanted the same for her children. Christmas was a magical time for Fritz and Gertrude. Weeks before Christmas the parlor doors were locked tight and preparations began. Arnold and Anna spent hours behind those locked doors decorating and wrapping presents. The anticipation for the children grew more intense every day as they sat just outside the doors and listened for any clues of the surprises to come. The best Christmas present Fritz ever received was an electric train set. For Gertrude it was a beautiful life-like doll and dollhouse. These gifts were put away after the holidays and brought out each year for Christmas. As Fritz listened through the door he would complain to Gertrude, "I can hear Papa playing with my train!" Finally, Christmas

Eve would arrive. The children were scrubbed clean and dressed in new Christmas outfits. As all their aunts, uncles, and cousins arrived, the anticipation grew more intense. After dinner everyone gathered around the piano to sing carols. By now the excitement for the children had built to a fever pitch. At long last the magical time arrived. As the parlor doors were swung open the children could see the spectacular sight of the decorated tree, full of candles burning, with presents spilling out underneath. Fritz's train was chugging around the room on its tracks and Gertrude's doll was sitting by her dollhouse waiting for her to play. The tree would be lit for that night only. As Fritz aptly put it, "We had the tree."

Life did seem ideal during those years. Little did the Wolf family know that an ominous cloud was forming on the horizon of their happy lives. Like the mythical Phoenix, Adolph Hitler was rising from the ashes.

Chapter 3

"Elect me and I will give you a Germany you won't recognize"

Adolf Hitler 1932

On October 29, 1929, the stock market in America crashed and the Great Depression spread over the entire globe. The results were disastrous for Germany. The prosperity of Germany came to a grinding halt. Millions were thrown out of work and bread lines stretched for blocks. Arnold was fortunate to have a job during those hard times; his family didn't suffer deprivation. But he and Anna were devastated for their country and worried what this new crisis would bring. Even though they still had work, like most Germans they couldn't relax. Fear of losing their job and going hungry was on every German's mind. The disastrous economy that they had only recently experienced re-emerged from their still scarred minds. Hopeless, hungry people were demanding a way out.

For Hitler, who predicted this disaster, the suffering of the German people was not a time to waste. "Never in my life have I been so well disposed and inwardly contented as in these days," he wrote. "For hard reality has opened the eyes of millions of Germans to the unprecedented swindles, lies, and betrayals of the Marxist deceivers of the people." In history most great revolutionaries succeeded only in desperate times. This would prove true for Adolph Hitler.

The ban on the Nazi party was lifted in 1927 and Hitler staged a rally that year in Nuremberg with 30,000 marching men. Even though the Nazi movement seemed benign, he was rebuilding his party and gaining momentum. He designed all-black uniforms and a style of marching copied from the Russians. Now, with the Great Depression, Hitler had his opportunity and intended to make the most of it. By 1929 the Nazi party had grown significantly, and Hitler staged another rally in Nuremberg this time with 60,000 marching men. During this year Hitler formed his notorious Schutzstaffel Storm Troopers, or the SS for short. Translated this meant protection squad. He put their members in special black uniforms and made them swear an oath of loyalty to him personally. At first, they numbered no more than 200 and were just a bodyguard for Hitler. They would grow into one of the largest and most powerful organizations in Germany eventually numbering over one million men and the SS became a name that would strike terror in all occupied Europe.

By creating what he called The Third Reich, Hitler wanted to place himself as successor to two great German empires and position himself in the large context of German history. He considered the Third Reich a conclusion to the process of German history tracing back to Charlemagne in 800. The term Reich (meaning realm) was not used by historians but had been coined by Arthur Moller Van den Bruck in his book, "Das dritte Reich," written in 1923. Lasting over 1000 years from 800 to 1806, The Holy Roman Empire, known also as The German Roman Empire, was named The First Reich by Hitler. Even though it was founded by the Pope in Rome, this empire was mostly German and continually ruled by German kings. Hitler saw himself resurrecting this great era of German history and ushering in another 1000-year Reich more powerful than the first. Because of Nuremberg's significance as a seat of power in the Holy Roman Empire, Hitler chose this site for his rallies. Most of the pageantry and symbolism from the empire was incorporated in the rallies. 1871 to 1918 was a time in history of unity for the German people called The German Empire. Again, Hitler saw this as a period of great German pride and named it The Second Reich. Hitler declared that Nuremberg would be the site of all future rallies which were to be held each fall.

Arnold and Anna must have had new concerns about the resurrection of the Nazi party. The impressive rally was held in the very heart of their city. It was evident the party was gaining momentum and Hitler was very clear about his goals if he came into power and of his hatred of the Jews. If his party ever took over the country it would stamp out individual freedom.

Adolph Hitler announced his candidacy for Chancellor of Germany on February 22, 1932. His party directed a campaign such as Germany had never seen. Colored election posters plastered the walls of buildings everywhere. Pamphlets and party newspapers were mass distributed. For the first time in an election, films and gramophone records were used. Hitler campaigned vigorously himself. Chartering a plane, he traveled all over Germany addressing three or four big rallies a day. He was a masterful orator and his speeches were described as "spellbinding." He promised the people a new and glorious Germany rescued from her enslaved state. He depicted a happy future if he was elected: jobs for everyone, a big army, booming business, and in one speech he went so far as to promise a husband for every German woman. "Elect me" he said, and "I will give you a Germany you won't recognize."

Hitler was defeated by a narrow margin in the elections of 1932. By then the Nazi party had grown significantly to about 400,000 members. In response to that growth, the Nazi party was banned after this election. Arnold and Anna must have breathed a sigh of relief at this news as Hitler had never hidden his intense hatred for the Jews. The German economy and government were in extreme turmoil after the election. As the government came to the brink of collapse, SS troops became part of daily acts of street violence. In 1933, the duly elected Chancellor of Germany, Kurt Von Schleicher, resigned and former chancellor, Franz Von Papen, reinstated the

Nazi party and appointed Adolph Hitler as German Chancellor. Few would have guessed in 1920 that by 1933 a ragtag gang of unemployed soldiers would become the new legal government of Germany or that a once obscure corporal, Adolph Hitler, would become the Chancellor of Germany, especially so soon after being defeated in a national election. Hitler had clearly stated before becoming Chancellor, "Once I really am in power, my first and foremost task will be the annihilation of the Jews".

Following Hitler's victory, he predictably began an intense propaganda campaign against the Jews orchestrated by what he called the "Reich Ministry of Public Enlightenment and Propaganda." Propaganda had been defined by Hitler: "Attempts to force a doctrine on the whole people, propaganda works on the general public from the standpoint of an idea and makes them ripe for the victory of this idea." Hitler's aim was to successfully communicate his National Socialist ideals including anti-Semitism through art, music, theater, films, books, radio, educational materials, and the press. During periods preceding legislation against the Jews, propaganda campaigns were heightened, designed to create an atmosphere of tolerance for violence toward Jews.

Hitler next formed The Geheime Staatspolizei (Secret Police). They were commonly referred to as 'The Gestapo," a shortened version of the formal name. The Gestapo was formed to investigate and combat all tendencies dangerous to the State and was restricted neither by law nor judicial review. They were specifically exempted from the court system and were given unconditional authority and the power to imprison people without judicial proceedings. At its peak the Gestapo had more than 45,000 members. Eventually the primary task of the Gestapo became to identity Jews and other undesirables for transportation to the concentration camps. They succeeded mainly because ordinary German citizens were willing to denounce one another and turn people in. To this day the name "Gestapo" is synonymous with brutal and unlawful acts of terror. In Hitler's eloquent speeches he mesmerized people into believing he cared for them and they were better off with him in power all the while cleverly deceiving them. The truth was they really had no rights. They had no political parties, no elections, no freedoms, and if another countryman turned them in to the Gestapo, no protection or right to a fair trial.

After he was appointed chancellor, Hitler immediately banned Jews from holding positions in the government. Although at this time, Jews were free to leave Germany, sadly very few did. The Nazi government soon made it almost impossible for Jews to leave Germany even though they announced to the press that Jews were free to leave. In order to leave, the Jews had to pay the Reich Flight Tax which was a very hefty amount, and agree to leave their homes and all their possessions behind. The Nazi government froze Jewish bank accounts so they could not access their money even if they wanted to leave. Even then, Jews wanting to emigrate had to find a country that would take them. The world seemed divided into two parts, those places where the Jews could not live and those places where the Jews could not enter. The only chance was if a relative in another country would sponsor them. The catch? The Nazi government had to approve the process.

Arnold and Anna wrestled with the decision to stay or depart their native country. One fateful day they sat down with their children and discussed leaving Germany.

It was a day that Fritz and Gertrude would always remember. The enormity of the decision was not lost on the children despite their young age. It scared them. How could they think of leaving their home and friends and all they held dear? Their parents had shielded them from the chaos around them and they did not grasp the danger they might face if they stayed. For Arnold and Anna, the decision was painful. It would cost them everything they had worked for to leave and, like most of the Jewish people in Germany, they thought that this madness could not last. Like many of their friends and relatives, they instead chose to live in an incredible state of denial. All around them Jews were persecuted and forced out of business, but they refused to see the handwriting on the wall. Arnold was fiercely patriotic and loyal to his country. Those Jewish men who had fought so valiantly in WW1 were convinced they were immune from Hitler's wrath. They felt their loyal service to their country would be honored. Arnold felt immune from persecution because he had defended Germany by risking his life. Many Jews still had jobs and thought they would not be deported if they were gainfully employed. Hitler used terms like "undesirables. . .lazy. . .and dirty" to describe the people being deported to the concentration camps.

Proud, hardworking Jews like Arnold could not comprehend that Hitler was casting them in the role of undesirables. Arnold was fiercely proud of his country. Germany had given the world the finest in science, music, universities, medicine, every field imaginable. The Jews had undeniably given Germany superb intelligence in all the fields of art and knowledge, research and economics. People of this great country would surely realize how crazy Hitler's rhetoric was and as fast as Hitler came into power, he would go out. Many Germans at this time simply thought the Nazi government would implode and didn't have a chance to succeed. Arnold still had his job, and no one knew or suspected he was a Jew and he really thought, like many well-respected Jews, that this would never affect him. Hitler was talking about lazy undesirable people not hardworking German citizens like Arnold. He and Anna weren't eager to leave their friends and relatives, or their beautiful home with all their belongings. Arnold's sister, Greta, and her husband, Sep, better understood the path Germany was on and with their daughter, Greta, abandoned their successful farm in the Rhineland and fled to France.

But Arnold, like many other Jewish men, continued to hope things would calm down and the worst was over. He, like most Jews, simply had no way to know what was coming. They made the decision to stay. That decision would haunt all four of them for the rest of their lives. Had Arnold and Anna known that one day the Nazi party would own all they had anyway and that their very lives would be at stake, surely, they would have raced out of Germany and not looked back. They simply were not prepared for the mighty force that was gathering against them. Hitler's well-oiled machine was now unstoppable.

By 1934, the Nazis numbered over 1 million. Hitler's troops were stationed all over Nuremberg and he continued to hold his impressive rallies in that city. In the rallies, thousands and thousands of soldiers marched in formation through the city streets. They looked formidable in their all-black uniforms and terrified little Fritz. Hitler had passed a law enabling him to bypass the Reichstag (government authorities) when making new laws. He had free rein with the government. His biggest supporters were big businessmen and industrialists who contributed a great deal of money to further the Nazi cause. During this year, Hitler became the Fuhrer (supreme ruler) of Germany and the German army swore allegiance to him. Hitler now had total control of the nation. He established Dachau outside of Nuremberg for undesirables and political prisoners. It was originally started as a labor camp but became one of the most notorious death camps in history.

By blanketing the German people with propaganda, the Nazis now brought anti-Semitism to a fever pitch. Hitler preached of a "pure Aryan race," which was superior to all other world races. He defined an Aryan as one of Nordic descent and not Jewish. He proclaimed that all people of true German or "Aryan" descent were true German citizens. This pure "Aryan" race was destined to rule all Eastern Europe. The Nazis identified the Jewish race as inferior and proclaimed, "The devil as the father of the Jew." They spewed hateful propaganda against the Jews that unfairly blamed them for Germany's economic depression and the country's defeat in World War I. Hitler maintained that if the inferior races mixed with the pure Aryan race the result would be the collapse of Germany. He appointed Josef Goebbels as his Minister of Propaganda. From then until his death, Goebbels used all forms of media--the press, radio, theater, films, literature, music and the fine art-- to further Nazi propaganda and instill in Germans their destiny as leaders of the world. Every form of media was controlled by the Nazi government. On May 10 of that year, he staged the" burning of the books" in Berlin. Works by Jewish and other "subversive" authors were publicly burned in large bonfires. Included were works by Albert Einstein and Sigmund Freud. The Nazis considered Einstein's "Theory of Relatively" a plot by the Jews to overthrow the government. The great Albert Einstein left Germany at this time with his wife Elsa. The United States offered him a position at Princeton University, sparing his life. Einstein later aided many Jewish scientists in their escape from Germany.

A flood of abusive literature aimed at all age groups was published and circulated throughout the country. The Jew was routinely portrayed as rat and vermin, a devil in human form. The literature went to such extremes as to brand Jews as murderers and pedophiles, dishonest and a blight on society. One popular children's book was titled, "The Poison Mushroom." It showed a boy and his mother gathering mushrooms in a beautiful German forest and was illustrated like a fairy tale. The boy found some poisonous ones. The mother explained that just as there are good mushrooms and poisonous ones, there are good people and bad people. The mother was proud of the boy when he explained that he knew that the poisonous mushrooms of mankind were the Jews. The mother praised the boy for his intelligence and went on to explain," Just as a single poisonous mushroom can kill a whole family so a solitary Jew can destroy a whole village, a whole city, even an entire folk." She also warned him that, "The Jew is the most dangerous poison mushroom in existence." This book was widely distributed even in classrooms. *Der Sturmer* (The Stormer) was the weekly Nazi newspaper and vehemently anti-Semitic. It often contained obscene anti-Semitic materials. It went to such extremes as to publish the statement that Jews slaughtered Christian children in their celebration of Passover and warned Germans to carefully watch their children that week. *Der Sturmer* was most famous for its anti-Semitic cartoons that portrayed Jews as ugly characters with grotesque facial features and misshapen bodies. The bottom of the title page always had the motto, "The Jews are our misfortune!" Hitler loved the paper and said it was "beyond question the most important weapon in his propagandist arsenal." Almost all illustrations of Jews in any of the media revealed features of stocky, misshapen bodies, bent posture, dark hair, bulging eyes, and large crooked noses. They were always covered in dark coarse body hair.

Every September the Nazi party held huge weeklong rallies that eventually brought hundreds of thousands of people to Nuremberg to view the extravaganza. Arnold and Anna watched in disbelief as their beloved city was showcased in newscasts and newsreels all over the world as newscasters descended on the town. Their charming medieval city would never again be known as, "The Jewel of Bavaria." It was now called the birthplace of Hitler and the Nazi party. The rally in September of 1935 would change the destiny of every Jew in Germany. Arnold, Anna, Fritz, and Gertrude would be thrown on an unimaginable path of pain and suffering. In just one day their lives changed forever.

The rally that September was a spectacle of pomp and circumstance, pageantry and mysticism with a religious-like fervor. The religion, though, was Hitler worship. Nuremberg prepared for the rally with festoons, signs, and swastikas all over town. The town was transformed from its quiet, medieval charm to a carnival like atmosphere. Frenzied crowds were everywhere, hoping to get even a glimpse of the Fuhrer. It was hard for Fritz and Gertrude to understand why they couldn't watch the parades and decorate their home like the rest of their neighbors. The other children on their street would proudly march in the rally in their Hitler Youth uniforms. They did not understand why their family did not simply hang a German flag in the window and join in with all their friends. All the children they knew belonged to the Nazi Youth Movement and they wanted to be part of that too. As the neighborhood children left for the meetings in their impressive uniforms, Fritz and Gertrude felt completely left out. Every child on their block belonged to the Hitler youth and to Fritz and Gertrude it looked like a fun exclusive club they so wanted to be part of. The Hitler Youth Movement was formed to educate children in the physical, intellectual, and moral spirit of National Socialism. It replaced all other youth clubs including Boy Scouts and church organizations. It eventually became compulsory for all German youth in the Reich. Parents who did not enroll their children could face imprisonment or the state taking their child away from them. The boys and girls in the youth movement always appeared happy and filled with an eagerness to serve the Nazi party. The clean-cut youth were growing up in the movement with strong healthy bodies and a love for their Fuhrer and country. As Hitler said, "He alone who owns the youth gains the future." For weeks their town was decorated and transformed but Fritz and Gertrude had to sit miserably in their house and miss the biggest party ever.

Adolph Hitler arrived by plane the night before the rally was to begin. His motorcade rolled slowly through the streets of Nuremberg lined with thousands of men, women, and children smiling, saluting, and cheering. Hitler stood in his car and smiled and waved at his adoring crowds. The crowd was in such a frenzied state of delirium at the sight of their beloved Fuhrer that SS men had to keep the people back. Mad loud cheering and chanting went on outside the hotel Hitler stayed at all night long. The crowds were shouting, "We want our Fuhrer," while fireworks went off overhead.

The rally officially started the next day in a large hall outside the parade grounds. 30,000 invited guests filled the great hall including members of the foreign press. Before the start of any rally a band would play "Die Meistersinger von Nuremberg" by Wagner, Hitler's favorite composer. Hitler strode in after the moving piece was played to the salutes and almost deafening chants in unison of "Heil Hitler." For many members of the foreign press it felt like a cult religious ceremony. In fact, it was hard to explain. To some extent, and nearly a hundred years later, it still is.

From the hall, formations of soldiers marched through the streets of Nuremberg with Hitler standing and waving in his car. People lined the swastika draped streets wildly cheering and saluting their Furher. The parade ended at the Nuremberg Stadium; a place erected expressly for the rallies. Here, Hitler strode in flanked by gigantic formations of Nazi soldiers. William Shirer commented that the finale of the rally was more than a gorgeous show; it had an air of mysticism and religious fervor. Hitler gave many speeches during the days of the rally but the rally itself culminated with a final fiery passionate speech by the great orator. In that speech, Hitler introduced the "Nuremberg Laws" which removed all citizens' rights for Jews. There were three important components to this law. The first was the "Reich Citizen Law" which stated Jews could not be German citizens and not claim equal citizenship rights anymore. The second was the component of the new law that defined who was a Jew. The third was the "Law for the Protection of German Blood and German Honor." This law forbade marriage between Jews and non-Jews.

Before this law was enacted, the Nazis had used several sometimes-absurd means to try to determine who was Jewish. They had equipment to measure body parts of suspected Jews and swatches of hair color to compare to their hair color. At one-point, Nazi scientists had determined a Jew could be recognized by his nose size and hair color. The Nazis had sought a legal definition of a Jew that identified them not by religious practices but by race. It was not easy to identify Jews in Germany as many were not practicing Jews and many had converted to Christianity. Now, for the first time the Germans had an official definition of a Jew that rejected the traditional view that Jews were members of a religious community but were instead a race defined by birth and blood. The new law defined a Jew as anyone with three or more Jewish grandparents or anyone with two Jewish grandparents who was a member of the Jewish religious community. A Mischlinge (half breed) was anyone that was part Jew. Mischlinges were labeled by degrees. A "Mishlinge First Degree" had one Jewish parent, and a Mischlinge Second Degree had one Jewish grandparent. Male first degree Mishlinges were considered full Jews. Arnold would be defined as a Jew and Fritz and Gertrude would become Mischlinges First Degree, a phrase they would come to dread. Eventually the rights of the Mischlinge would be continuously curtailed through legislation. The Nazis in their usual, orderly fashion meticulously checked every German's background by this criterion. Tens of thousands in Germany who were not tied to a religious or cultural Jewish community were surprised to find themselves newly classified as Jews. Those who did not practice Judaism assumed the criteria would be based on religious preference and would not affect them.

These new laws set Jews apart from Germans legally, politically, socially, and economically. They foreshadowed the dark path Hitler was leading his people down. This cruel, sinister path would forever scar the history of the German people. The German people, though, were drunk with adoration for their leader and happy with their new prosperity. Thus, they believed their leader could do no wrong. As they raised their hands in salute to Hitler that day in Nuremberg, they would have been shocked to realize that this very city would soon lie in ruins and their beloved Fuhrer would die a coward's death. But much pain, suffering and death remained before those fateful days.

The Nuremberg Laws had an immediate effect on all Jews and lives were drastically changed. For the Wolf family their change in status was immediate. Fritz and Gertrude, unaware of the new law and what it meant to them, went to the bottom of the street to join their friends as they always had to walk to school. But now all the children ignored them and refused to walk with them. Gertrude realized something was wrong with her and Fritz for the first time. She was shocked when the one of the boys told her: "It's too bad you are not Aryan; you are a Jew!" It was news to her. Neighbors who had been their closest friends began ignoring them and snubbing them. They would deliberately turn their backs on the Wolf family when they saw them or go into their homes and close the door behind them. The same thing happened to Fritz when he went out to play with his friends. Before that they did not realize that all the propaganda directed at the Jews included them. They saw the banners all over town with ugly pictures of Jews and derogatory words. It was impossible to grasp that they were those Jews. Now they knew they were not pure Aryan and were thus inferior and enemies of the people.

Both Gertrude and Fritz started to feel worthless and isolated. They bought the lie that there was something inherently wrong with them. When I asked my Aunt Gertrude many years later how people knew her father was Jewish, she replied: "They had a way of knowing, people had a way of knowing everything." Gertrude remembered only one neighbor on her entire street that tried to be kind to her and Fritz. He would go out of his way, even cross the street, to talk to them and ask how they were doing. That small act of kindness stayed with her all her life. The children in the neighborhood were not allowed to play with Fritz and Gertrude anymore. It was impossible for them to understand why their very best friends suddenly hated them. One girl in particular would spot Gertrude or Fritz outside and incite the other children to taunt them and throw rocks at them. They went to school and came home only to play by themselves. Before they were classified as half Jews and not pure Aryan, they had had friends over every day to play and were invited to all the neighborhood birthday parties. In a swift and frightening turn of events they became hated and rejected, subject to an onslaught of cruel words and treatment. Leaving the house became a nightmare.

Now Arnold and Anna were breaking the law by being married to each other and were in danger of being arrested. The Nazis were trying to force Aryans of mixed marriage to file for divorce. Soon, the situation for Arnold and Anna became frightening. Aryan women married to Jews or dating Jews were called "Jews' Whores." Acts of violence against these women were occurring frequently and publicly. Three members of the foreign press as well as the American ambassador to Germany witnessed such an incident in Nuremberg. They went to see why a crowd of some 2,000 people had gathered around a street tram in the center of town. As they watched, huge men in brown uniforms removed a young woman from a tram. Her face was smeared with white powder, her head shaven, and her blond braids pinned to a placard around her neck that read, "I have offered myself to a Jew". They led her through lobbies of hotels and crowds in the streets. When she stumbled they lifted her to her feet. The crowd cried, "Speech, Speech" and they lifted her to their shoulders for everyone to see. The young girl, an Aryan named Betti Suess, had been discovered in the arms of her Jewish fiancé. Herr Streicher the mayor of Nuremberg was behind the spectacle. This story was reported in *The New York Times* as well as *The London Times*. The story at first caused enormous outrage in the foreign press but propaganda

Minister Goebbels excused the incident as isolated and unimportant. *The New York Times* later reported that Betti Suess was taken to an insane asylum, her mind broken by the humiliation. The incident was soon forgotten, and the foreign press did not report on it again. They may have deluded themselves that this was an isolated incident, but it was in fact commonplace in Nuremberg. This was the environment that Anna, married to a Jew, found herself. It became increasingly dangerous for Arnold or Anna to leave their home. Anna could not venture out alone; she always had members of her large family accompany her and she and Arnold had to be careful never to be seen in public together.

All Jewish businesses in Germany were boycotted. Arnold and Anna saw large Stars of David painted in yellow and black across doors and windows of businesses in their city. Signs were posted on the buildings "Do Not Buy From Jews." One non-Jewish businessman who was interviewed after the war was asked if the boycott of the Jewish businesses in his town bothered him at all. He replied that he was in fact glad to see them boycotted as it meant more business for him. Other businesses displayed signs, "Jews Not Welcome Here." I have often wondered what my grandfather thought as he walked the streets of

Nuremberg with anti-Jewish signs and posters plastered everywhere. After all, he himself was a Jew as well as his family. Did he finally realize the enormity of all of this? By now he was not free to leave Germany as he had a big J (for Jew) stamped on his papers. How hard it must have been to remember the day he made the decision to keep his family in Germany. If only he could turn the clock back.

School soon became a nightmare for Fritz. Right away his teacher moved him to the very back row of the class because he was Jewish. At first the children just ignored him. They wouldn't play with him or talk to him. Eventually it turned mean. German children indoctrinated and desensitized by anti-Jewish propaganda were eager to brutalize their Jewish peers. The kids threw rocks at him on the way to school and taunted him by calling him a "Dirty Jew." They would form a circle around him at recess and hit and kick him. He would run to the bathroom and hide by standing on a toilet in a stall for his safety during recess and lunch and try to take different ways home to avoid the turmoil. It is interesting that it was not just a few bullies, but all the children who joined in this cruelty. His teachers, who had always praised him and helped him in school, joined the cruel taunting or turned their backs on it and ignored it. For Fritz the hardest part was trying to understand why they hated him so vehemently. These were the very friends who had come to his birthday parties, played at his house, and with him on the playground at school. Because his family did not practice Judaism or attend Synagogue, Fritz had no concept of what it meant to be a Jew. He could not understand that it was not about religion-- Hitler wanted to destroy an entire race of people. Fritz hurt inside from all the cruelty and hatred. He became afraid to go outside his house. It used to be exciting to go to the town square and shop with his mom and watch the trains. Always his neighborhood had been a fun and safe place. Now he knew he would be taunted wherever he went, and he was terrified of the Nazi soldiers standing guard all around his town. He was forced to stay inside his house and play all alone. At the end of the school year that would have been the equivalent of fourth grade, school became unbearable for him. He came home one day and said, "I can't go back." He was not yet 11-years-old. By now he had been taunted and tormented for a year and a half. His parents respected his wishes as they knew he loved school and wouldn't quit unless it was indeed unbearable. Fritz feared for his life. He knew he could be beaten to death and nobody would come to his aid; in fact, they would pride themselves on the act. Many Jewish children dropped out of school at this time due to the persecution and violence against them. It was a triumph for Hitler as he said it showed that Jewish children were lazy and stupid. A group of boys from the Nazi Youth was always lying in wait watching for Fritz to leave his house, ready to pounce on him and beat him up. Fritz finally refused to leave the house at all. He said they would just as soon kill him and consider themselves heroes and sadly, he was right. By now, Fritz was having horrible nightmares. He would wake sweating and trembling always thinking that the Nazis were after him. Hardest for him were the unanswered questions. Why did everyone hate him? What had he done wrong? Why was he Jewish? His parents could not help him with questions they did not understand themselves and they could do nothing to soften the heartbreak. The worse part for Fritz was that he started to believe he was in some way deficient and undesirable. Arnold and Anna hopelessly watched as their beloved son, who had always been happy and outgoing, became depressed and withdrawn. Lonely and frightened, he spent all day every day at home working on the schoolwork his parents planned for him and playing with his toys. Even his beloved train set was brought out in hopes of cheering him up but although he enjoyed it, he was still sad and lonely. The carefree days of his childhood were over.

By the spring of 1938 Jews were not allowed to have electricity or gas for their homes. Also, that spring, the Nazi party set up concentration camps for what they called "undesirables." This included any Jew guilty of even a minor traffic violation. Soon "undesirables" were defined as those Jews not working or not in school. The Nazi party portrayed them as lazy and a drain on the economy. This was the same government that had stripped them of their jobs and right to go to school. To Fritz this was absurd. He wanted nothing more than to attend school and learn. The Jewish men without work wanted desperately to work; they were not lazy. They loved their families and their country and were complete innocents having done nothing wrong. These camps were really slave labor camps. The people worked under harsh conditions to build roads, dig out quarries, shovel snow, or any number of back breaking jobs.

They never returned home; they were literally worked to death. To the Jews it likely seemed that things could not get worse. But, of course, they did get worse.

Anti-Jewish Propaganda

"When the vermin are dead, the German oak will again flourish."

Jews not served here

Hitler Youth Rally

Nuremberg Rally 1935

Newspaper announcing
Nuremberg Laws

Chapter 4

"Germany allowed itself to be robbed of its conscience
and its very soul"

Charles Dubost *1938*

On March 12, 1938, German soldiers marched into
Austria which was then annexed to Germany. The
190,000 Jews in Austria became subject to all German
laws. The Nazis were faced with what they called a
"Jewish Problem" that called for more effective
measures; efficiency counted for everything while
humanity counted for nothing. And so, after the
annexation of Austria, the persecution campaign against
the Jews of Germany and Austria intensified. Jews were

required to carry identification cards, each with a large "J" stamped on it. Failure to produce the card was punishable by death. New laws against Jews were passed almost daily; by 1938 more than 400 such decrees and regulations were in effect. Seemingly, no area of Jewish life was overlooked. The Germans must have worked night and day to think of laws against minor things such as buying cut flowers or woven cloth. All professions were eventually forbidden to Jews. Jewish doctors and lawyers could no longer practice. Jews could no longer own businesses, and businesses they did not own could not employ them, and Jews could not teach. All Jewish businesses were dissolved. Jewish children could not attend school. Jews could not own drivers' licenses, were not allowed to own radios, and could shop only between 4 and 5 p.m. The list of anti-Jewish laws was endless. Even street names with any association to Jewish background were changed. It became impossible for a Jew to legally work or earn money in any way. The depth and breadth of the anti-Jewish campaign is nearly inconceivable today; in fact, there are those who would deny these practices existed. But the historical records are plentiful and beyond question.

Arnold and Anna were caught in the middle of this madness. Where Anna was free to leave the house and shop where she wanted, Arnold could only go to town for a short time each day and could not shop at most stores. Soon there would be sections of town Arnold could not enter, and only one piece of a public park he was permitted on. He had to be careful to be in public only during the allotted time and walk and shop in only those few areas left open to Jews which were constantly shrinking as more and more places were declared off limits. How could anyone keep track of it all? For Anna's safety they never ventured out in public together. It had to be hard for her to be a free citizen while her husband was subject to such harsh laws. They watched in horror as the scenario unfolded before their very eyes. Arnold could not be easily identified as a Jew just out walking the streets of Nuremberg, but he, like all citizens, had to always carry his identification papers, his with the dreaded "J" stamped on them. If he broke any of these laws, he was at risk of being asked to show his papers. The fear of swift punishment kept Arnold and other Jews from trying to hide their papers or break the laws.

By late November of 1938 Jews could not attend cinemas, theaters, or concerts. They were allowed in public areas only one hour a day. They could buy food only in specialty shops. They were to relinquish all their valuables to the Nazis with no compensation in return. They could not bear arms. An entire Nazi publication titled, "The Jewish Newsletter," was needed simply to keep citizens apprised of current regulations regarding Jews.

In June of 1938 the *"Asozialen-Aktion"* (Action against Anti Socials) was passed. All previously convicted Jews; even those with only minor traffic offenses, were arrested and deported to concentration camps. Classified as Anti Socials were Jewish men twelve and over who were not working or in school. Since Jews were forbidden to work or to attend school, few were spared this hideous fate.

In May of that year Fritz was lonely, frightened, and frustrated but still refused to leave the house. He became more withdrawn and despondent. His parents were concerned not only for his mental health but for his safety because they knew he would be conscripted to a Nazi labor camp in August when he turned 12. Horror stories of the camps had begun to surface and terrify the people who remained at home. In fact, the leak of the stories was intentional because the Nazis wanted to scare citizens into compliance. The Jews in Germany were trying to navigate bewildering new circumstances. How could anyone cope with such insanity? Because he was not attending school Fritz would be classified as an anti-social, lazy, and a blight on society. The once bright, ambitious son who thrived in school and thirsted for knowledge was forbidden to attend school and because he wasn't a student, he was classified as an anti-social. By now nearly all Jews were in the same predicament. None could work in their professions: doctors, lawyers, teachers, professors, store clerks, even farmers were forbidden to work and were denied jobs. They were then classified as lazy and anti-social and deported to camps.

The Nazis had subtle ways of making cruel laws seem sensible by their titles: "The law for the protection of German blood and honor" or the "Law against crowding of German schools." The "Anti-Social Action Law" sent all these people to camps by declaring them lazy and an enemy to the country even though other recent German laws were responsible for making them seem that way.

The Germans were unrelenting in closing every door to every Jew. Such efficient and total ruthlessness has not often been seen in the history of man.

A solution to the family's immediate problem came when Arnold's sister, Grete, offered Fritz a job working on their farm in France for the summer. Grete and her husband, Sepp, owned a working farm named, "The Guensbach Farm," in the Moselle district of France, near the German French border. A plan was made to somehow get Fritz across the border into France to Sepp and Greta's farm. Everyone believed it would be just for one summer. Even with a 95 percent citizen approval rating for Hitler and a rapidly deteriorating atmosphere for Jews, Arnold and Anna clung to the hope their situation would improve. It would be risky to try to take their son out of Germany because, if they were caught, it meant certain and immediate deportation for Fritz. Anna applied for a travel visa to visit relatives in France for Fritz and her. By an absolute miracle the travel visa was approved; somehow the usually 100% efficient Nazis missed that he was not allowed to travel outside Germany. Fritz was terrified as he left for the train station with his mother. He had said an emotional goodbye to his father and sister, and he knew, even at the young age of 11, this was a risky venture. He trembled at the sight of the Nazi soldiers all around them at the train station; to a young boy they looked like frightening giants, barking orders and demanding allegiance. His mother dutifully saluted and said, "Heil Hitler" and made Fritz do the same. This surprised him since he had never once witnessed his mother salute a Nazi soldier. One can only imagine what she felt as she betrayed one set of values for another. Miraculously, after she presented their papers they were allowed on the train. (When I visited Nuremberg with my father sixty years later, stepping into that very train station brought back memories for him of that frightening day. He still expected to see Nazi soldiers standing guard all around the train station.)

That train ride seemed to last an eternity. Fritz expected the train to be stopped at any time so that he and his mother could be sent back to Germany. It was a massive relief when the train pulled into the station in France without incident. People were milling around in normal fashion and there was not one Nazi soldier to be seen. For the first time in years, Fritz felt safe. It was refreshing to see a place free from swastikas hanging on every building, or horrible anti-Jewish posters at every turn, or "No Jews Here" posted on businesses. He and his

mother were free to travel to his Uncle Sepp's farm
without fear of harassment or possible arrest. Of course,
as we who have the benefit of historical perspective well
know, France as a sanctuary for Jews was relatively short
lived. Many of the terrors for Jews that existed in
Germany would be transported to France during the
German occupation.

Anna snapped a quick picture of her son with Sepp
and Greta before she turned to leave. That picture would
bring her comfort and hope during the long years of
separation from Fritz when she didn't know if he was
even alive. It helped her cope with her desperation and
anxiety by looking at his dear face and telling herself she
would hold him in her arms again someday.

Even though he was frightened to leave his family,
he consoled himself by thinking this was just one
summer; besides, he thought it might be kind of an
adventure to work on his uncle's farm. Gertrude thought
her big brother was just going for a short visit with their
mom and was devastated when Anna returned without
him. It was hard on everybody but the toughest problem
the family had faced was solved with Fritz finally safe in
France. Everyone realized a miracle had occurred and

their gratitude for his safety overshadowed their despair. Arnold and Anna thought that by summer's end this lunacy would end. They were sure they had taken Fritz to the farm to help just for the season's harvest. Little did Arnold realize he would not see his son again for nine long years. The miracle was that he would see him again at all.

Fritz, who had been the beloved, pampered son of his parents was now a farm hand living with the farm help. His uncle wanted him to keep a low profile and not call attention to the fact he was on their farm illegally. Since they lived just over the border from Germany they still feared for Fritz's safety. They had him live and work with the hired help so neighbors would think he was just a new employee. The work was grueling. It was hot that summer and Fritz found out he was allergic to hay. He spent the summer sneezing with red swollen eyes; with every chance he got he submerged his head in a bucket of cold water for relief. The hired men were kind to him, and he was grateful to have friends again. They helped him learn the tasks of farming and included him in their activities at night. Fritz learned to work hard and long hours and was becoming strong and muscular; he later reported that he could work as hard as a grown man which might be something of a young boy's exaggeration but there is no doubt, he earned his keep. In August of that summer he turned twelve. His first eleven birthdays had been happy celebrations with his family. That year he spent his birthday working in the fields. He was so homesick that he toyed with the thought of just walking away from the farm all the way back to his family. For his own safety communication was cut off from his birth family so he worried about them probably as much as they worried about him. But it could not be helped. Unsettling reports of the chaos in Germany were pouring into France daily. Any communication between Fritz and his family almost certainly would have been intercepted by the Nazis who would have stopped at nothing to get him back under their control. So, while "radio silence" was painful there was no safe alternative.

Finally, the summer of 1938 came to a close. "Now," Fritz thought, "I can go home." He waited anxiously for his mother to return to France to take him home. His dream was shattered when his uncle explained to him that Germany was still too perilous for his return and, at the same time, his mother could no longer travel safely to France.

It had been a long summer; he was so tired and homesick that he just wanted this madness to end. Unfortunately, his nightmare was just beginning.

Chapter 5

"The opposite of love is not hate, it is indifference."
Elie Wiesel

By the fall of 1938, things were spiraling out of control
for Arnold and Anna as well as for all Jews in
Nuremberg. In August of that year Nazi troops destroyed
the beautiful Jewish Synagogue in Nuremberg and
burned it to the ground. On November 9, 1938, the Nazis
unleashed a wave of violence against Jews all over
Germany. It was a night of terror as Jewish shops and
synagogues were destroyed. Hitler's SS troops and every
day and otherwise normal German citizens smashed the
windows of Jewish businesses with sledgehammers. The
events became known as Kristallnacht (Crystal Night), or

the night of the broken glass. Centuries old synagogues were burned or left unrecognizable. Prayer books, scrolls, and artwork were taken from the synagogues and burned in the streets. Even graveyards were not spared. Tombstones were uprooted and graves violated. Jews were dragged in the street and beaten to death. On that single night 100 Jews were killed and 30,000 were arrested; 7,000 Jewish shops and 1,668 synagogues were destroyed. Every synagogue in Germany was either damaged or destroyed. Kristallnacht changed the nature of persecution of the Jews. Previously it had been economic, political, and social persecution, which was bad enough. But now it became physical with beatings, murders, and incarceration. Kristallnacht is often referred to as the beginning of the Holocaust. On November 10, a rally was held in Nuremberg with more than 10,000 people in attendance to celebrate the success of Kristallnacht.

As Arnold and Anna walked through Nuremberg after that night, they were heartbroken. Their beautiful city was in shambles. They wondered how Arnold's boyhood home and family business had fared. Even though Marie no longer owned the business Arnold worried it too had been destroyed. Kristallnacht was a wake-up call for both Arnold and Anna. They realized the Nazis were out of control with their hatred of the Jews and they were unstoppable.

After November 9, 1938, the Nazis implemented a plan to make it yet easier to identify Jews in public. All Jews over 12 years of age had to wear a white armband 4 inches wide with a blue Star of David on it. The Jews were required to buy and distribute the armbands, and the star, as intended, created discriminatory isolation for the Jews and promoted even worse persecution.

Gertrude hated walking with her father with his armband on. As they walked through the streets people turned away, or mocked them, or sometimes spit on them. She felt so ashamed to be on the streets with her father that she eventually refused to walk with him. Later she regretted her actions, but how could a 10-year-old girl understand any of this? All she knew was that people who once were friendly and smiled on her as she walked with her father now treated her with utter distain.

Soon a new insignia was created--a patch with a 6-point yellow star with the word Jude (Jew) written on it in black. The age of accountability was lowered again and now all Jews six years of age or older were required to wear the patch on the left side of their breast and on their backs. Jews became shattered and despondent as their lives became more miserable in public. It became known to many Jews as the star of shame. Later it made it easier to identify Jews for deportation to concentration camps. Only one month after the new patch was introduced mass deportations began.

In December of 1938 a law was passed barring Jews from owning a home or a car. Landlords were required to cancel any lease to a Jew. Juden haus (Jews houses) were established for Jews to live in. They were small, run-down apartments that became mini slums. The Germans used the word "ghetto" to describe them, a word we use to this day. Families were packed into the apartments and shared one kitchen and one bathroom. A tiny two-bedroom apartment might have twenty people living in it.

Arnold lost his job and the Nazis forced his family from their beautiful home. As they told it later, one terrifying night there was a loud pounding on their door. The Gestapo had surrounded the house. Gertrude remembers shaking with fear as the men arrested her father and took him away. The men gave Anna and Gertrude a few minutes to gather up a few belongings and leave the house. The Gestapo spread out through the house. Each soldier had a clipboard and as was the usual custom of the meticulous Nazis, documented every item they owned. Their beautiful home and all their earthly possessions now belonged to the Nazis.

Anna and Gertrude were left standing on the street each holding a bag with their meager belongings. They had no idea where the men had taken Arnold. As Gertrude clung sobbing to her mother, Anna had to calm the frightened child and figure out what to do next. The vivid memory of the day that they sat in their home and made the decision to stay in Germany would forever haunt her as life came crashing down in a split second. Anna had to navigate her way in a bewildering and confusing situation. The unthinkable had happened; the Nazis had it all, even Arnold.

Anna's sister, Gustie, was alone in her a small apartment with her husband away at war. When Anna and Gertrude showed up on her doorstep, she welcomed them in. They would soon find out that Arnold had been taken to a Juden Haus in Nuremberg and Anna set out to find him. She found Arnold living in one room with several men in a small crowded apartment. Arnold was confused by the arrest. He, like many veterans of WW1, had thought his service to his country would protect him. Many Jewish men brought their medals from the war with them with when they were called to report to the Nazis. They would plead with the men showing them the evidence of their love and sacrifice for Germany. Arnold was fiercely patriotic and loved his country but none of this mattered any more in Germany. Any Jew, even one who willingly and gallantly had defended Germany, was considered less than human and a parasite by the pure Aryan people.

Anna had to find work to support herself and Gertrude. She became seriously depressed during this time and lost her zest for life. The fun-loving mother that Gertrude had always known was gone, Anna would never completely recover from the trauma of those years. Not only was she separated from her beloved son, the Nazis had her husband as well. She had lost her beautiful home, all her lifelong friends, and the lifestyle she loved and now she and Gertrude were destitute. Life became a drudgery of trying to find work while living with Gertrude in the living room of her sister's small apartment. Despite all this, Anna had a resilience that the Nazis could not touch. She would use her intelligence and resourcefulness and find a way to outsmart the Nazis and save her family.

It was urgent that Anna find somewhere to hide Gertrude. Gertrude was ten now and growing into a beautiful girl with blonde hair and blue eyes, the coveted "Aryan look." Hitler preached that the perfect race, the Aryan race, had blond hair and blue eyes. It was to Gertrude's advantage that she did not look Jewish like her brother did, but the Nazis would soon be after her. Anna's biggest worry was that her daughter's beauty would invite the Nazis to rape her. So, she took Gertrude to live in the country with her sister, Freida. The people in that small village did not know that Anna was married to a Jew. Gertrude, with her blond hair and blue eyes fit in as a typical Lutheran girl so she was able to attend school and make friends again. Nobody snubbed or ridiculed her. Always in these hard situations the family thought everything would end quickly and return to normal. Gertrude certainly did not imagine that she would be living with her aunt for six more years. Later in life she would share that she felt abandoned by her parents. Many Jewish children wrestled with feelings of rejection and abandonment. They simply could not understand the dire circumstances their parents faced nor could they comprehend the heartbreak of the Jewish people. Parents faced impossible choices: keep their children with them or send them to an uncertain but safer life. After Kristallnacht, the Kinderstransport was organized. England had listened to the pleas of the Mennonite society that begged them to rescue Jewish children aged 2 to 17 from the Nazis. Thousands of children were taken by train from Germany to England and saved from certain death. Sobbing children were literally torn from the arms of their mothers and put on the trains. Older children were given the younger children to care for on the journey. Hitler allowed the children to leave until 1939. It was heartbreaking. Others, like Gertrude, were taken to safer places and hidden with relatives or friends. Parents had to leave their children in the hands of sometimes complete strangers and hope against hope that the Nazis would not find them. Most children never saw their parents again. Ninety percent of Jewish parents chose not to send their children away and instead opted to keep them with them not realizing they would all eventually be deported to the camps. Gertrude was lonely and homesick and felt like a burden to her aunt.

She was fortunate to be hidden and protected from the Nazis for such a long time, but they would eventually find her as well.

Anna risked everything and moved in with Arnold in the Juden Haus. Perhaps she felt she could protect him by living there or maybe she just missed him. She was willing to live in the squalor of the Jewish ghetto to be with her husband. Life in the Judan Haus was hard. People, hungry and desperate, lived on the edge of insanity. By now the Jews had very few freedoms. They were not allowed to work or buy or sell. The Nazis would gladly have them all starve to death. At any moment, just to be cruel, a Nazi soldier would come to the apartment simply to torment them. The soldiers would burst in the apartment spouting obscenities about the Jews and threatening them with deportation. They were free to abuse them physically as well. Often, they would take some Jews to the town square to publicly ridicule them. They would cut off a beard in public, which was especially humiliating for a practicing Jew, or force them to scrub the cobble stone streets on their hands and knees, or crawl on the ground and eat grass. It was fun sport for the Nazi soldiers as well as the townspeople who laughed and applauded enthusiastically. Every day whole families were rounded up and taken away to a holding area in preparation for deportation. Juden Hauses were always located by train tracks to facilitate the transport of people to the camps. The train would pull into the designated area and empty box cars would be opened. Nazi soldiers forced the people into the cars, pushing and prodding them with their rifles and whips while the frightened and hysterical people pleaded for mercy. Parents separated from children in the pandemonium became desperate to find them. As mothers screamed for their children and husbands and wives called for each other the soldiers kept prodding the people and loading them on the cars. The soldiers would push and shove more and more people into a boxcar. It looked like no more people could fit but they would still force more people on. Each time a boxcar was filled the door was shut and tightly bolted. The small air holes in the doors were covered with bars and barbed wire. The people near the door were the fortunate ones. They had air to breathe. Many in the rear of the cars died from lack of air. As the trains rolled away desperate screams could be heard over the engine noise. People in each Juden Haus lived in constant dread as they witnessed this scene over and over— when would their turn come? There was a desperate certainty that it would. No one among them any longer had hope. The Nazis had extinguished all light in their lives.

Just a few short years earlier Arnold and Anna had been on top of the world. Arnold was a German citizen, respected for his service to his country. They owned a beautiful home, had two handsome children, Arnold had a promising career, and they had many friends. Now they were living in poverty and squalor. Fear was a constant companion and Arnold could be deported without warning at any time. With the election of Adolph Hitler, this was the story for every Jew living in Germany or Austria. The Nazis had expanded Dachau and added three more concentration camps in Germany and one in Austria. They were concentrating on a solution to "the Jewish Problem," as it was now called. Jews were moved from the countryside as well as throughout the cities to large cities and held in ghettos near railroad transportation so they could be easily transported to the concentration camps.

Germany invaded Poland on September 1, 1939, starting World War II. France and England had a defense pact with Poland and declared war on Germany and the

Soviet Union on September 3. Germany and the Soviet Union crushed Poland's resistance and occupied it by September 17th. It was a swift victory. Germany occupied west and north Poland and the Soviet Union, east Poland. Two million Jews who lived in Poland thus came under Nazi rule. The German people were surprisingly cavalier as the radio and newspapers announced the invasion of Poland and the declaration of war by Great Britain and France. Foreign reporters covering the news in Germany were caught off guard by the attitude of the masses. The German people had so much confidence in Hitler and the victories seemed so effortless, they may have thought they would easily and painlessly conquer Europe. After all, Hitler had promised them that was their destiny. Sadly, World War II would become the most widespread and deadliest war in human history. In Germany alone, 5,533,000 soldiers would lose their lives along with more than two million civilians.

In October of that year Hitler enacted a euthanasia program for what he defined as "useless eaters." The operation was given the code name "T-4". The people classified as "worthless" were physically or mentally disabled children and adults in Germany and Austria. Hitler deemed them a blight on Germany's racial integrity and an economic burden to the state. Those condemned to die were transported to centers in Germany and Austria equipped with gas chambers disguised as tiled showers. Statistics show that 70,000 to 80,000 people were murdered under this plan. Operation T-4 proved to be the blueprint for what would become "The Final Solution of the Jewish Question."

In early 1940 all the men in Arnold's apartment were arrested and taken with other Jewish men to the holding area in preparation for deportation. When Anna found the apartment empty, she frantically searched for Arnold and found he had been taken to the deportation area. Fortunately for Arnold, Anna was, as noted above, a very clever woman who had been working on a backup plan in case Arnold was arrested.

She had earlier been in contact with Latter-Day Saint family members in Salt Lake City, Utah. Anna's aunt had converted to what was then called Mormonism in 1900 and her entire family migrated to Salt Lake City. Anna had begged them to help get her family out of Germany. The aunt, along with her religious community, had raised a good sum of money to help get them out and somehow had gotten it to Anna's relatives in Germany. Anna had a brother and brother-in-law who were Nazi soldiers, so she had connections to the Nazi guards. It was hoped that it was enough money to get the entire family out of Germany. But with Arnold ready to be deported, the guards took all the money as a bribe to let Arnold go. He was secretly whisked out of Germany to Italy; from there he was put on the last passenger ship to leave Europe until the war was over.

Later some people without much knowledge of history or the specific situation criticized him for leaving the country without his family; those who are more knowledgeable of German history of the time realize it is impossible for those not living in that environment to understand the situation he was in. Under a death sentence in Germany, he had no control over either the bribe or his escape. He could have refused to board the ship but that would have meant certain death. He could not help his family escape if he was dead. But even knowing those things, as the ship slowly left the port and headed to the open sea, he must have been overcome with sorrow at the realization that he was leaving his family behind in the hands of the Nazis. He surely thought he could get to America and find a way to bring his family to safety, but the curtain closed quickly. How he must have wished he had left Germany with his family in 1933 when he had the opportunity; but at that time, he didn't want to leave his country, lose his home, or lose his job. Now he had lost everything. The Nazis had it all.

The Yellow Star

All subjects in these pictures were deported to camps.

Kristallnacht

Synagogues were
destroyed

Businesses were destroyed

Jews were paraded through streets

Chapter 6

"Final Solution of the Jewish Question"
Meant the complete extermination of all the Jews in
Europe."

Rudolph Hoess

"I do not know what a Jew is.
I only know human beings."

Andre Trocme

Fritz was unaware of the turmoil his family was facing in the fall of 1938. To ease his homesickness, he daydreamed of returning to pre-Nazi Nuremberg where his family would be waiting for him with open arms. No children tormented him, there were no Nazi soldiers to frighten him, and all the ugly anti-Jewish posters and banners were gone. He dreamed of Christmas celebrations, and dinners with long discussions with his parents, and long walks through Nuremberg with his father. "This too shall pass" became his mantra. This absurdity would end, and everything would be back to normal. How he missed his carefree childhood! But, of course, that was his dream and it was incredibly far from the reality that faced him then and would continue to face him in the future. He would be forced to witness things no child should have to see.

By May of 1940, the job for Fritz that was supposed to have lasted four months had stretched into two long years. In the meantime, Sepp and Greta had rescued another nephew, Ernst, from Germany who was working with Fritz on the farm. It was good for Fritz to have a friend his own age living on the farm and, as we might expect the two boys formed an incredibly close bond. Homesickness was a constant companion with birthdays and Christmases the hardest and those were things boys would share. However, as the months stretched into years, Fritz' dream of returning home seemed impossible. News reports from Germany were more and more discouraging and disheartening. He constantly feared for his family's safety and did not know if they were even alive. Communication remained very dangerous at both ends. The Germans had proved very adept at finding those who had escaped their nets.

Eventually Fritz would learn that his family had lost their home and his father had been rescued and was, everyone in the family hoped, safe in America. Things in Germany had become worse for his family not better, and as a result his dream changed. Germany became the hated enemy rather than the beloved homeland and he now pictured himself returning home only to rescue his mother and sister and bring them to America which became the place of hope and freedom in his mind. He planned to leave Germany with his family and never look back. He told himself over and over, "I WILL join my father in America." He had a new hope and vision and clung to it even when the dream seemed impossible.

France was on edge that spring. Hitler had annexed Austria and invaded and captured Czechoslovakia and Poland. His goal was to conquer all Eastern Europe. He also had his eyes on France and seemed unstoppable.

Germany invaded France on May 10, 1940. Paris fell on June 14 and by June 25, just 46 days later, France surrendered. The lightning speed of the sudden surrender by France shocked the world. The truth of the matter was that France had been woefully unprepared for the German war machine. With an army of adequate size, France had felt prepared, but they were to face a German army with highly sophisticated tactics and advanced weapons.

The defeat for France was swift and humiliating. As part of the surrender treaty France agreed to sacrifice all its Jews to the Germans who quickly occupied the country and almost immediately Jews were subjected to the same anti-Jewish measures as in Germany. According to the terms of the surrender, the French could set up a puppet government at Vichy in the southern part of France. The Vichy government was given the equivalent of 2/5's of France and under the agreement it would remain unoccupied by the Germans. Because there were no German soldiers stationed in the Vichy area thousands and thousands of Jews fled to Southern France. In all more than 150,000 Jews crossed the demarcation line hoping for protection from the Nazis. Sepp and Greta took Fritz and Ernest with them as they joined the mass exodus bringing with them only what they could carry. They started the long, arduous trek south leaving their farm and everything they owned to the invading Nazis. Those poor refugees did not know that the Vichy government had voluntarily collaborated with the

Germans, agreeing to hand their Jews over to the Nazis. The Vichy government enacted the exact laws Germany had against the Jews and required them to wear yellow arm bands as well. In a cruel twist of fate those Jews fleeing the Nazis were arrested and put in internment camps as they flocked into Southern France. The camps, under French control, became dismal prisons for the weary refugees. Living conditions for Sep, Greta, Fritz, and Ernst were harsh. They had little water, no electricity, no toilets, no privacy, and very little food. It was miserable existence and they soon realized they had not escaped the Nazis after all. In May of 1941, mass arrests were made of all Jews in the Vichy region and they were thrown into the camps. Conditions became crowded and even more unbearable. Sanitary conditions deteriorated, and the prisoners, dirty and hungry, now lived with fleas, mice, and rats. Many died from starvation and disease. Soon the Jews from what became known as transit camps were being transported by cattle trains to the German death camps. The transit camps were put there solely to make deportation to Germany easy and efficient. In one camp in France, Gurs, 15,000 Jews were imprisoned by 1941. Of those only 48 remained in August of 1943. Of the 75,000 Jews deported from France between March 1942 and August 1944 only 4000 returned.

Heroes emerged from the horrors. As the Vichy government began mass arrest and deportation of Jews, an underground movement called the Oeuvre de Secours aux Enfants--Children's Aid Rescue Society, or OSE-- organized a network for the protection of Jewish children. The organization set up homes in four villages in southern France to house children they smuggled out of refugee camps. The OSE was the largest communal effort of its kind in Europe and rescued an estimated 6000-9000 Jewish children in France prior to 1944. Unfortunately, the system was far from foolproof. As early as August of 1942 the police had begun raiding OSE houses and deporting Jewish children.

George Garel was one tireless worker who helped to set up an organization inside the OSE to rescue children from the homes before the Nazis could find them. The Circuit Garel as it became known worked to place children they rescued in farms throughout southern France because they were safer places. Ordinary people risked their lives to hide these Jewish children. Food was scarce and they sacrificed to feed and care for them.

Another hero was Pastor Andre Trocme who, when asked to hand over Jews, replied: "I do not know what a Jew is. I only know human beings." One farmer said years later that he protected the Jewish children because it was the right thing to do.

Fritz and Ernst were rescued before they could be deported to the death camps and taken into this underground system. They were taken to a safe house in a village in southern France where they were well taken care of, a welcome relief from the deplorable conditions of the refugee camp. Fritz would learn years later that his Aunt Greta had died of an illness in the camp and his Uncle Sepp had been deported and gassed to death in a concentration camp.

A kind farmer and his wife in southern France eventually offered to hide Fritz and Ernst in their barn when they needed rescue from the OSE house. They were an older couple living by themselves. Enough cannot be written about those brave people, "The Righteous Gentiles," who put themselves in grave danger to hide Jews during WWII. They risked their own lives to save complete strangers, beacons of light in this dark, dark time. One of those men who hid a Jewish family was later interviewed and asked why he would risk his life to hide a complete stranger. His reply was that he would rather lay his head down on his pillow in peace than lay his head down at all. What if all the people of Germany or France had been so brave? Those people who selflessly hid the Jews at great cost to themselves were some of the unsung heroes of the Holocaust. There was a farmer in southern France who was willing to hide my father and his cousin. We will never know his name or what happened to him and his family. Did they eventually die or go to prison for their bravery? That was the penalty for hiding Jews. Several dozen employees and more than 100 supporters of the OSE paid the ultimate price when they were murdered by the Germans for rescuing Jewish children.

Like many of the children rescued, Fritz was confined to the loft of a barn. Children were hidden in cellars, attics, closets, barns, even sewers. It was a hard, lonely life for these children as they endured isolation and the immeasurable grief of separation from their families and, for that matter, everyone ese. Since strict secrecy was required, they could have absolutely no contact with their parents, something Fritz was pretty much accustomed to by now. Most of the hidden children became orphans because of Hitler's obsession with killing their parents. They faced constant fear and danger, always terrified the Nazis would find them. Many times, they had to stay perfectly still and quiet for hours and hours. Fritz fought despair by again telling himself, "This too shall pass." Knowing it could not last forever was his only link to sanity. He would repeat the line over and over like a mantra and hope against hope that everything would go back to normal someday. Of course, normal for him had changed to life in America which he continually vowed would be his destination in life. In addition to the fear for his own safety, he was worried sick about his mother and sister. Did the Nazis have them? Had they escaped? He could only think of them as alive or he would lose his mind. To be so completely cut off from his family was as bad as the lonely isolation. He felt as though he could endure anything if he only knew they were safe, and that he would see them again. The Nazis had taken so much from him, his family, his education, even his self-esteem. But they could not take away his hope.

Germany invaded the Soviet Union on June 22, 1941, breaking the German-Soviet pact signed in 1939. Germany was now immersed in a two-front war. After the invasion, Hitler sought a solution to the Jewish question once and for all. Never in human history had the mass slaughter of an entire population simply based on their race been attempted on such a scale. Mass murder of the Jews had become an official state policy after the invasion. On July 31, 1941, Hermann Goering gave the order." I hereby instruct you to make all necessary preparations as regards organizational, financial, and military matters with a total solution of the Jewish question within the area of German influence in Europe." The order had been signed by Goering, Hitler, and Adolf Eichmann. That summer the mass slaughter of Jews began. Special mobile killing squads called the *Einsatzgruppen* were established to rid Hitler of the Jewish problem. As the Germans marched in and occupied new territories, shooting massacres of the Jewish population began. The elite troops would round up thousands of Jews, have those who could work dig massive ravines, then have the people strip, lie face down in the ravine on top of corpses and shoot them one by one in the neck. There was no distinction between men, women, and children. All were killed. These massacres were documented on paper with pictures attached. There were detailed diagrams of the ravines to be dug. In these disturbing diagrams, dead corpses lie in the bottom while a person kneels ready to be shot and fall dead into the ravine. The sadistic Nazis took pictures of naked women begging for their lives on the way to the ravine. The soldiers seemed to take great pleasure in humiliating their victims before they were shot. Although the Nazis later tried to cover these atrocities up, many supporting documents and pictures still exist. The pictures are a shocking reminder of their heartless cruelty. For example, one document from Kiev is dated September 29 and 30, 1941. During those two days alone, 33,771 Jews were shot to death in the ravine outside the city. That year, the 3,000-member special units shot 1.3 million Jews to death, one by one.

In June of 1941 the Nazis started experimenting with mobile killing units. Gas vans with hermetically sealed trucks used engine exhaust diverted to the interior. Gassing proved to be less costly and more efficient that shooting. By September they had discovered that Zyklon B pellets became deadly when converted to a lethal gas. The first experiment with Zyklon B was conducted at the Auschwitz concentration camp in Poland by gassing 600 prisoners of war and 250 ill prisoners. Auschwitz became the first large scale killing center. Full operation of extermination camps began. At the height of deportations 6,000 Jews were gassed each day at Auschwitz alone. The Nazis built the gas chambers to resemble large showers. As the trains entered the death camps the people were herded off the cattle cars and paraded in front of SS doctors. Those who looked able to work were put in one line and those deemed unfit to work--mothers, children, pregnant women, the old, and the sick--put in another. The able-bodied were taken to work camps. Those who remained were put on lorries and taken to be gassed. Unaware of the fate that awaited them they were told they were being taken to the showers to be disinfected. Disguising the gas chambers was an important step in keeping the victims calm and enabling the process to proceed smoother and faster. Fake dressing rooms were designed with numbered pegs for people to hang their belongings. Signs with slogans like "Lice Can Kill" and "Wash Yourself" pointed the way to the chamber. The victims were even given a sliver of soap. As the victims approached the door, they were ordered to enter the showers with their arms raised high to allow as many people as possible to fit in the chamber. The Nazis had camouflaged the gas chambers well with fake plumbing and fake shower heads in the ceiling. After the door was shut and sealed the gas was released. People panicked when they realized what was going on and clawed their way to the door, banging on it and screaming to be let out. Nazis watched the whole wretched scene from a window and didn't open the doors until there was no sign of life. Rudolf Hoess was among the many SS guards who witnessed the gassings from a peephole and wrote detailed descriptions of the effect of the gas and the reaction of the victims for the benefit of the Nazis. Even though the Nazis attempted to destroy all evidence of their evil deeds as the allies closed in, much evidence still remained. The German penchant for accurate and complete records was their undoing since they were unable to destroy those records in time to save themselves from discovery and later prosecution. Included were diagrams and pictures of the gas chambers with detailed charts of the number of people killed each day as well as descriptions of their victims' deaths in the chamber. At first the victims were buried in mass graves. Later crematories were constructed, and the bodies burned in them. This system allowed them to gas 6,000 people in a single day.

As early as the end of 1941, mass deportation and slaughter of the Jews had begun. Germany now occupied

Poland, Norway, Belgium, the Netherlands, Luxembourg, Greece, Yugoslavia, and France. Japan had bombed Pearl Harbor and America was now in the war allied with England and the USSR. Among Hitler's primary goals were to control all of Europe and to annihilate all of Europe's Jews. In every country Germany conquered he established concentration camps. The deterrent effect of the concentration camps was based on the promise of savage brutality which was fulfilled to an extreme that defies description. Once in custody of the SS guards, the victims were beaten, tortured, starved or murdered through the "extermination through work program," mass executions, or any means that happened to be handy. If there was a way for one human being to exhibit extreme cruelty to another, the Nazis, under Hitler's directive, found and employed it.

Those who were chosen for the "extermination through work program" faced unimaginable conditions. Hunger and starvation, sadism, disease, beatings, and shootings were accepted treatment for prisoners who were required to work inhumanly grueling days with little or no food. The Nazis stood over them and beat them if they felt they weren't working hard enough or being respectful enough, or just because they felt like beating them. If a prisoner could not work, he was shot in the neck and carted off. If someone was sick and could not get out of bed for formation in the mornings, he was shot and removed from the barracks.

In 1942, mass deportation of French Jews began. The Nazis made a concerted effort, as they had elsewhere, to locate all Jews in France. Generous rewards were offered to anyone who would identify a Jew. Farmers were under constant surveillance and any suspicious activity was reported. One cannot begin to imagine the intense fear the farmer's family was living with as long as Fritz and Ernst lay hidden in their barn. They could easily have given the boys to the Nazis and kept their family safe. They would even be heroes to the Germans. Or they could have just told the boys to leave and fend for themselves. But in the face of adversity they bravely kept Fritz and Ernst hidden in the loft of their barn knowing it could cost them their lives.

On April 9, 1943 the unspeakable happened when the French police, in collusion with their Nazi occupiers, raided the farm. In the middle of the night Fritz and Ernst were awakened by the sound of screeching tires and loud voices. Obviously tipped off by an informant, the police went right to the loft of the barn and arrested Fritz and Ernst. The two terrified teenaged boys were taken at gunpoint to a waiting car and whisked off. It happened so fast the boys did not have time to try to escape or see if the farmer and his wife were also arrested. They were taken across the border and handed over to the Gestapo in Trier. Fritz was booked into the Trier prison where another nightmare was about to begin for him.

Chapter 7

"Whatever happens, the flame of the French resistance must not be extinguished and will not be extinguished."

Charles de Gaulle
June 18, 1940

Fritz and Ernst were taken across the border to Trier where they were handed over to Nazi soldiers. As inmates arrived, the Nazis happily shook hands with the French police and congratulated them on the arrests; the atmosphere was almost jovial. With the stakes high, and rewards generous, who knows how much the French police received for turning over two Jewish boys.

As the French police drove away, the tone changed, and the guards barked orders at Fritz and Ernst and pushed them to a brick building barely illuminated in the night's darkness. They were booked into the Trier Prison on April 9, 1943 and separated right away.

The Trier Prison was established in the nineteenth century in the town of Trier, Germany, and because of its convenient location near the French border, it was used by the Nazis to imprison political prisoners arriving from France. It was a relatively small facility with 84 cells and prisoners were kept there for a short time while they were interrogated and then transported to various camps. By 1943, prisoners were arriving daily and due to the crowded conditions, they were crammed into cells with standing room only. With no room to lie down or stretch out sleep was impossible and the stench of the portable toilet in each cell became unbearable.

Right away the Schupo (Nazi protection police) started interrogating Fritz. What was he doing in southern France? Why was he there? Fritz had no idea why they kept asking the same questions over and over again. He kept telling them he was a farmhand and nothing more. Day and night, he was brought for interrogation and taken back to his dismal cell. Prisoners were fed one slice of bread with a bowl of watered-down soup each day at noon for their only meal. Hunger, fatigue, and mental exhaustion were the weapons of choice to break the prisoners down. What Fritz didn't realize was that he was suspected of being part of the French Resistance. While he had been in a refugee camp and hidden on a farm, he was unaware of the heroic movement to thwart the Nazi German occupation in France that was operating all around him. The interrogators asked the same questions over and over trying to get information on a topic Fritz had never heard of. The futility of it all frustrated both parties. Fortunately, Fritz could not reveal information he did not know so was of no assistance to his German interrogators.

The French Resistance began in southern France when the Vichy government openly began to collaborate with the Nazis. It is a story of common people who did extraordinary things. In France's darkest hour ordinary citizens refused to accept the degradation of human values and banded together to form one of the greatest mass resistance movements in history. Men and women from all economic levels and political leanings, Jews included, came together to form resistance cells. The

Resistance, of course, was in direct violation of the armistice signed by France. In the beginning the Resistance consisted of a few small cells of men and women who wanted a means to fight the German occupation of France. By using sabotage tactics such as cutting power lines, vandalizing Germany military vehicles, and disrupting communication lines, and by publishing underground newspapers, they worked to disrupt the German programs. As the Resistance grew larger, they built and maintained escape networks for Allied soldiers trapped behind enemy lines, blew up bridges, and derailed trains. Eventually they began to kidnap and kill German officers.

The Nazi government classified them as terrorists but despite that, the movement gained momentum as the people of France were faced more and more with an atmosphere of fear and repression from the Germans. Many cited the brutality they witnessed by the Nazis as their inspiration to join. For others the savagery against the Jews and the deportation of French Jews to death camps caused them to join. The Resistance became a vital part of the rescue of Jewish children, backing and helping The OSE (Ouvre de Secours aux Enfants) rescue effort and many others as well. Individuals associated with the

Resistance movement rescued hundreds of children single handedly. Among them was George Loinger who is credited with the rescue of hundreds of children by means of getting them across the border to Switzerland. The great mime, Marcel Marceau, was also a member of the French Resistance and is himself credited with saving hundreds of children by leading entire orphanages of Jewish children across the French border. He said his ability to mime, and keep the children entertained, helped to keep them quiet during the perilous journey. By 1943, all able-bodied French men and women aged 20-22 were required to work in Nazi labor camps. Soon all able-bodied men and women aged 18 to 45 were required to work in the camps. This caused many to flee the Nazis and join the Resistance. To fight the Resistance the Nazis issued a "Code of Hostages" that called for the murder of ten innocent Frenchmen for every Nazi killed. All district chiefs were required to draw up lists of people to be executed. On October 20, 1941, 50 innocent people were executed for the retaliation of the murders of two prominent Nazis in Nantes. On October 23, another 50 were executed in Nantes when the perpetrators did not surrender, and 50 more were executed that same day in Bordeaux for the murder of a prominent Nazi there. As the conflict escalated, the number grew to 50 innocent French for every Nazi murdered and eventually that number reached 100. Despite much debate and controversy, the Resistance refused to concede, stating that it would be a win for the Reich if they did. The Nazis by then were executing citizens for acts of sabotage as well. Because of Resistance activity in the vicinity, the entire village of Oradour was razed and almost every resident was murdered. An estimated 30,000 people were executed by the Nazis in retaliation for Nazi officers killed or acts of sabotage.

And yet, in spite of the tremendous risks, the Resistance movement aided the Allies in the invasion of Normandy by providing the Allies with intelligence on German defenses and carrying out acts of sabotage and is given major credit for helping to make the operation a success. Eventually the movement would have over 400,000 members. Of these, 56,000 were captured and sent to concentration camps; only half of those survived. Even though these ordinary citizens did not set out to be heroes, they emerged as great symbols of bravery in Europe's darkest hour. General and later President Dwight D. Eisenhower, the Supreme Allied Commander of the Allied Expeditionary Force, said that without the help of the French Resistance Movement the liberation of France and defeat of the enemy in Western Europe would have consumed a much longer time and meant infinitely greater losses.

Hoping to gain inside information on the Resistance Movement, the interrogators continued the questioning almost non-stop. Terrified by it all, Fritz could only repeat over and over that he knew nothing and was just a farmhand. He had no way of knowing that his fate was sealed no matter what he said and that he would be deported as either an escaped Jew or as a Resistance fighter or maybe even both. Not satisfied that he knew nothing of the Resistance, his captors ordered that he be transferred to Nuremberg where he was booked into the Nuremberg jail on April 14. It was, of course, ironic that the Germans sent him to his hometown even though it was entirely different from when he had left.

Almost five years to the day from when he left with his mother to go to his uncle's farm in France, Fritz was back in Nuremberg. He was back where he dreamed of returning but with a cruel twist of fate since he had never imagined himself a prisoner in the Nuremberg jail. He was close to his mother and sister but so far away. Were they still in Nuremberg ? If only he could walk out of those doors and find them. The frightening interrogations continued day and night. Why was he in France? What was he doing there? What did he know? Over and over he answered, "I was just a farmhand," but the Nazis were never satisfied.

Anna learned from inside sources that her son was in the Nuremberg jail. He was alive and in Nuremberg, but the most dreaded thing had happened: the Nazis had him. She had done all she could to keep her family safe and for five years she had been successful. Her shrewd planning and quick thinking had kept her husband and children from the Nazis. Now they had her beloved son and it seemed the Nazis had won. In a brave and desperate move, Anna went to the jail to plead for the life of her son. She swore her allegiance to the Nazis and told them she had left her husband and denounced his Jewish faith. Please free her son, she begged, because he had done nothing wrong. How frustrating it must have been for her to stand outside the prison knowing that her son, whom she had not seen or heard from for five long years, was inside that very building. What did he look like? Where had he been? How did the Nazis find him? Oh, to see him, to touch him, to hear his voice again!

In an unusual move the Nazis relented and allowed Fritz to see his mother. One can only imagine the joyful reunion of mother and son. The boy Anna had said goodbye to so many years ago in France was now sixteen, almost a man. There was so much to catch up on. He had only heard bits and pieces of his family's story at first while he was working on his uncle's farm in France and later had no communication with them or about them at all. Now his mother was able to fill him in on all that had happened during his five-year absence. It was hard to listen to the story of how the Nazis had seized their home and arrested his father and taken him away to a Juden house. But it was a huge relief to learn for sure that his father had narrowly escaped deportation and was in America. It made him sick to think of the Nazis living in the boyhood home that held such precious memories. Gertrude was living with their aunt and uncle in the country and able to attend school. How did the situation in Germany spin so out of control? In return, Anna learned of Fritz's escape to southern France and of the kind farmer who rescued him from deportation and sheltered him in the loft of his barn. The fates of Sepp, Greta, and Ernst were unknown. Knowing his life was in the hands of the Nazis, their time together was bittersweet. He was not a free man.

The dreaded orders for deportation came. Cleverly disguising the fact that Fritz was going to a concentration camp, the Nazis told him he would be working in a factory. Sheltered all those years in France, he had little knowledge of the Nazi atrocities or the conditions of the camps. Anna knew. Word was out that the Nazis were gassing people who could not work and those who could work were subject to inhumane conditions and eventually worked and starved to death. Not one person who had been deported had ever returned. Deportation was a death sentence.

On May 13, 1943, Fritz again found himself in the Nuremberg train station. This time he was there with hundreds of people being shoved and pushed onto a train by armed soldiers. There was only room to stand in the cars by the time the train left the station and armed guards were all around them. As the train pulled away from the station, he was unaware that he was riding the train from Nuremberg to France. The first trip was to escape the Nazis but this one was as a Nazi prisoner. The Nazis had not told him that he was being deported across the border to Natzweiler, the only Nazi concentration camp on French soil. The irony of his returning to France, again on a train, is nearly over whelming in retrospect. And our narrative thus returns once again to French soil, the country that Julius Caesar described as divided into three parts. Alas, occupation by the Germans was nothing like occupation by the Romans had been centuries before. The Romans used existing infrastructure; the Germans destroyed it.

Cover of prisoner's
book from Trier
Prison

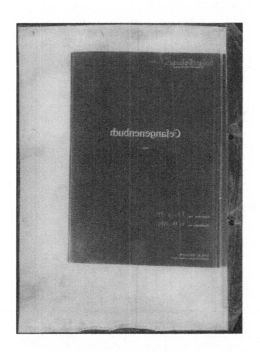

From the prisoner's book Trier Prison

The page where Fritz Wolf is listed under prisoner #56
2nd column gives date and time of his incarceration, April 9, 1943.
3rd column gives his name, date, and place of birth and his profession as   farm hand.
4th column shows the enforcement authority: States Police of Trier
Last 2 columns give date and time of his discharge and reason for it: Transfer to the police jail of Nuremberg. April 14, 1943.

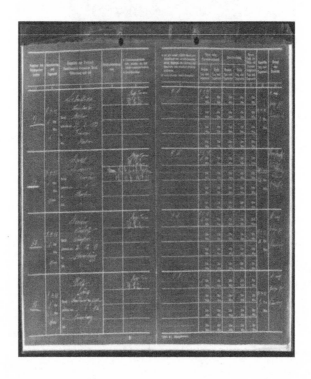

Cover of the prisoner's
book of the police jail
of Nuremberg

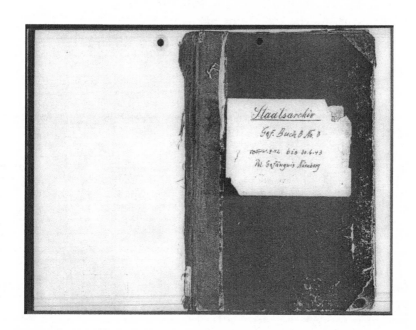

The page of Nuremberg book of the police jail where Fritz is listed under number 1600.

In the 2nd row under his name his profession is given as worker.

The next columns detail: his date of birth; place of birth; marital status; religion (deistic); reason for incarceration(protective custody;) accompanying documents(trans port docket); admitting authority (mayor of Trier); Date of his admittance (April 15, 1943); Date of end of his arrest(May 13, 1943)

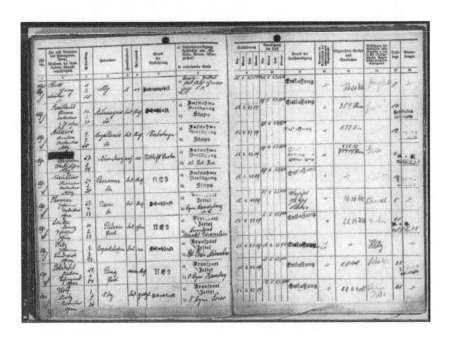

Chapter 8

"We weren't even human to them.
We were like ants to be played with and destroyed at
will."

Fritz Wolf

The train sped into France and stopped at the Alsace station. Prisoners were herded off the train and, weak, tired, and hungry, forced to hike five miles up a 2,500-foot mountain to the camp. They were chased up the hill by armed Nazis and vicious dogs, the Nazis yelling, "Schnell! Schnell! Schnell!" (quickly, quickly, quickly) a word they would hear constantly from that point on in their captivity. They were marched through the town of Natzweiler while people peeked through curtained windows at the pitiful sight of the flagging prisoners. Before any prisoner train arrived, Nazi soldiers went throughout the town ordering everyone off the streets. One prisoner recalled a woman wiping a tear as she watched the forced march. Many prisoners were simply shot on the spot because they were too weak or weary to make the forced march. As those remaining in the main body of prisoners approached the main gate they were met with an astonishing sight; a beautiful mountain villa complete with a swimming pool. The villa was the cruel and sadistic camp commander's residence sitting just a few hundred meters from the camp. The stunning mansion stood in tragic contrast to the stark ugliness and utter madness of the camp. As the prisoners arrived at the entrance, they faced an immediate and terrifying sight: electric fences, observation posts, and an enormous metal gate. Above the gate the sign read Konzentrationslager Natzweiler-Struthof (Concentration Camp Natzweiler-Struthof). By now Fritz knew that this was not a factory job. Any panic or resistance was met with whips and guns. As the gates shut behind them, the prisoners were marched into the very pit of hell. The sign above Dante's version of Hell in *The Divine Comedy* would have been an appropriate addition: "Abandon all hope ye who enter here."

Taken to a holding room they were stripped of all their clothes, shaved, forced to take a cold shower, and then de-liced. After being issued their prison clothes and wooden clog-like shoes, they were given numbers. No longer would they have names but would just be numbers. Taking away a person's name was and is a particularly cruel way to dehumanize and humiliate a prisoner. A name is personal and holds much significance for a prisoner. It sets that person apart and makes them unique, and it is wholly and completely their own. By reducing them to numbers, the Nazis made sure their prisoners knew they were not human to them, each merely a number in the labor force.

On the other hand, numbers rather than names made it easier for the Nazis to distance themselves from any personal attachment to prisoners since numbers have no real identities. From the main processing center these now "identity less" prisoners were divided into "identity less" groups and taken to one of the 55 subcamps where their nightmares intensified.

The Nazis established the Natzweiler concentration camp in the province of Alsace in Eastern France. Built in 1941 in the beautiful French Alps it was the only Nazi concentration camp constructed on French soil. Natzweiler was in the town of Stutthof, a popular ski area until 1940 when SS geologists discovered a vein of valuable pink granite in the hillside. Himmler ordered the area off limits to the public and in 1941 started the construction of a forced labor camp to mine the granite.

Natzweiler was originally built to subdue the growing number of anti-German resistance fighters in France. Those who were suspected of being resistance fighters were classified as Nacht and Nebel (Night and Fog) prisoners. The name comes from the fact that they simply disappeared into the night and fog with not even their families notified of their fate. Perhaps the most famous documentary film of all time was titled "Night and Fog" (1956) and memorialized some of the events described herein.

Originally Natzweiler was a small camp with only 7000 prisoners who were to be worked to death under a sentence of hard labor. The first prisoners constructed their own prison under brutal conditions. The SS never stopped pushing the starving work teams. When a man was ill or unable to work, he was simply shot. After the completion of the prison barracks and buildings, the prisoners were forced to dig underground quarries in the hard granite. These underground caves were used to house sheds serving as workshops for building and overhauling airplane engines. In the same area, deep tunnels were dug underground for subterranean factories hidden from the enemy.

In 1942, when Albert Speer, in charge of the Armament Ministry, decided to relocate much of Germany's armament production to underground factories, hidden from the Allies, Natzweiler became one of the camps designated for the purpose and construction of camp annexes linked to the war industry. Eventually there were more than 50 sub camps. By 1943, in addition to resistance fighters, other prisoners were brought to the camp from all over Europe. Lebenstraum is a theory, usually associated with Nazi Germany, that a certain amount of territory is needed for natural development of a country; Hitler used this notion to justify German expansion and occupation of the countries that surrounded it and it was an important component of Hitler's ideology. He believed living space for the

German population should come from Eastern Europe. This policy allowed for the economic exploitation of conquered territories. Hitler felt the inferior, conquered people should be killed, deported, or enslaved to make room for the superior Germans. Accordingly, once Germany had conquered a country all males were conscripted into unpaid slave labor and taken away. Eventually as Germany needed more laborers for the war effort, women and children were also kidnapped and taken to labor camps. The method of choice for disposing of these unwanted people was the "Annihilation through Work" program. The orders were, literally, to work them to death.

By the time Fritz was conscripted to the forced labor camp it was filled to more than three times its capacity. Huts constructed to house 150 people now had 650 to 700 living in them. Prisoners were sleeping three to a bed. The Germans thus had compelling reasons to work more people to death than usual and, thus, Fritz was in greater jeopardy than he otherwise might have been. He was not only unwanted and detested but also redundant. The supply of workers now exceeded the demand, or, least, the Germans ability to house, clothe, and feed their work force.

The total number of prisoners at Natzweiler and its sub-camps is estimated to have been 52,000 over the years it was in operation. Strenuous work, medical experiments, poor nutrition and mistreatment by the SS guards resulted in an estimated 25,000 deaths from 1941-1945. Natzweiler had a far higher death rate than other comparable Nazi labor camps which earned it the title "City of the Dead". It is remembered as the little-known Nazi concentration camp with a sad history. In reality, it was a place where the Nazis systematically murdered about 120 innocent people each week for four years.

Fritz would spend the rest of his life trying to understand the cold-blooded brutality of the Nazis at that camp. Later he said, "We weren't even human to them. We were like ants to be played with and destroyed at will." He said that you could not be that cruel if you thought you were dealing with human beings. The savagery of the Nazis would prove impossible to grasp.

For young seventeen-year-old Fritz, the misery of the camp defied description. Conditions were brutal and hunger and sleepless nights took their toll. Sleep was almost impossible in their rat-infested housing. Exhausted from a long day's labor Fritz would fall into a deep sleep only to be awakened by bone chilling screams all around him. Rats were eating the flesh of those who had fallen asleep. Soft areas of the body, like ear lobes, were especially vulnerable. Nighttime became a nightmare of trying to stay awake to avoid the rats while at the same time desperately needing sleep.

Morning came early and started yet another long brutal day. One sink with only cold water was available for washing which was done half naked and quickly under the watchful eye of the guards. Prisoners received a pint of what the Nazis called "coffee." Afterward they were marched to roll call where the guards counted each man. If a man was missing, a search began while the prisoners waited. If someone slept through roll call or was too sick or weak to report they were shot to death. Even though the main camp had a gas chamber and ovens, Fritz remembered the victims were brought out naked in front of the prisoners, shot to death, and thrown into a mass grave. No doubt this was done to frighten and torture the men who were forced to watch the cruel fate of their fellow prisoners. After roll call Fritz would begin his work shift in the underground armaments plant making ball bearings for aircraft. A traditional German second breakfast was served midmorning which consisted of bread sometimes accompanied by a small amount of margarine or tiny slice of sausage. At noon a watery nondescript soup was served. On Sundays a few pieces of meat were added to the soup. Dinner consisted of "coffee" and bread with a small amount of cheese or a spoonful of marmalade. Historians know exactly what was served because the Nazis kept meticulous records in that camp; they noted, for example, that a person could survive on the equivalent of 400 calories a day. Although the Nazis tried to hide the atrocities of the camp by destroying records as the Allies closed in, some documents survived. Hunger was Fritz's constant companion though he was hardly alone with that problem. The scant amount of food served each day barely kept the teenager alive. Hunger drove the men to constantly talk or dream about food. Studies done on starvation corroborate anecdotal evidence. There was little time or interest for camaraderie among the prisoners. Survival was all that mattered and it was an individual thing. Most moved through their long, hard day like robots, just trying to make it one more day. If a man stopped talking about food or lost interest in food, it was a sign he had given up and the others knew he would soon be dead.

Fritz continued to tell himself over and over, "This too shall pass." He had to believe someday this would end or he would give up like many others already had. His mantra again got him through the worst days. He would dream of his family and envision their joyful reunion. The winter he spent in the high French Alps at the camp was an especially harsh one. During the long morning roll call, sometimes lasting several hours, he was forced to stand perfectly in the bitter cold without a coat, causing frostbitten fingers and toes. That winter was the hardest for him and the time he became the most discouraged. Cold, tired, and hungry, he nevertheless managed to trudge through each day barely making it through. Many others, of course, did not, 25,000 of them.

Hardest for Fritz to deal with was the constant harassment and brutality of the guards. All day long they hurled insults at their prisoners, never letting up. Prisoners were beaten mercilessly or shot on the spot for the smallest infraction of the rules, which were many. When addressed by a guard they had to look at the ground and answer humbly and respectfully. Never were they to look a guard in the eye. Their tormenters tortured them for sport and laughed at their pain and misery. He would ask himself over and over, "Why do they hate us so much? What did we do?" Man's inhumanity to man has been wrestled with for centuries with no satisfying answer. Fritz decided that there was no way to comprehend the Nazis' mindless cruelty. He bought the lies of the enemy telling him he was the scum of the earth, worthless and not fit to live on the earth. His self-esteem was already fragile from the years of harassment and torment from his teachers, classmates, neighbors, and especially the Hitler youth who kept him a prisoner in his own house. The Nazis had convinced him something was inherently wrong with him. It was a pit into which he was thrust that would take years to climb out of.

We might well ask how a sensitive seventeen-year-old survived such a hell hole. He lived in absolute filth, dealt with constant hunger, fatigue, and was always at risk of being beaten or shot. The guards were sadistically cruel, taking delight in tormenting their victims. They would beat a man at will or shoot someone in the neck just for sport. Fritz witnessed day in and day out the utter disregard for human life. People were tossed in a pit like everyday garbage. He lived in a rat-infested hut, had only a quick wash at the sink every day, and lived in ragged dirty clothes. Hungry, filthy, and tired with no relief in sight, he trudged through every day confident this too would someday pass. He said he was never afraid the Nazis would kill him; he never thought he would die in that camp. Because of his confident belief that he would survive, and life would get better, he could endure the very pit of hell. This too shall pass. This too shall pass. It would get better; it certainly could not get worse. Thoughts of his family motivated him to get up each morning and brave another dismal day. Now that he knew for sure they were all alive, he had a renewed hope that they would all survive this insanity and be reunited again, hopefully in America with his father. The love of his family, the warm memories of his early childhood, and the hope of a better future kept him from giving up. Despite the endless madness, he still believed someday it would end and he would be a free man again. This could not, would not last forever.

Natzweiler

Entrance to underground factory

Chapter 9

"I opened the door and just like that, there he was! "

Anna Wolf

By June of 1944 Fritz had been a prisoner in Natzweiler for just over a year, but to him it must have seemed an eternity. Conditions had deteriorated rapidly as the Nazis brought more and more prisoners to add to an already overcrowded camp, and death and disease were rampant. Fritz faced each day hungry, exhausted, and filthy with no idea what day of the week it was because the schedule every day was exactly the same as the days that had gone before. Still he kept on going, even when it looked hopeless. For a lesser person it would have been easier to let the Nazis win the battle for his life but somewhere deep inside him, he found the will to live, ever mindful that many others in the camp had given up and chosen death as a welcome reprieve for the misery they had endured. Using a strategy that today is often called suicide by cop, some stayed in the barracks at roll call, preferring to be shot to death rather than report to work. Thoreau once said that most men lead lives of quiet desperation; never was that notion more applicable.

War was raging all through Europe by now, but the prisoners knew only the madness of the microcosmic world in which they lived, denied any news from home or the outside world. They did not know that the Allies were planning one of the largest military operations ever staged and France would soon be liberated. Had they known, of course, more would have retained the will to live but in this area, too, the Germans were successful in stifling that basic human urge to survive, probably the strongest of our individual and collective instincts.

On Tuesday, June 6, 1944, now referred to as D-Day, thousands of paratroopers landed behind the scenes in the pre-dawn darkness and more than 156,000 troops from America, Britain, and Canada stormed 50 miles of beach in Normandy, France, in what would become the largest seaborn invasion in history. The Germans had prepared for the attack by fortifying 2,400 miles of beaches with bunkers, land mines, and beach and water obstacles. General Dwight D. Eisenhower called the operation a crusade in which "we will accept nothing less than full victory." The cost in lives of D-Day was high with more than 9,000 killed or wounded, but by day's end the Allies had secured the beaches and begun the liberation of France and eventually all of Europe. By June 11 all the beaches were secured, and more than 326,000 troops had landed in Normandy. They were eventually joined by 850,000 additional troops and began their march across France. As they fought their way through the landscape of the French countryside, they were met with determined German resistance, but the Allies forced the Germans to retreat. All over France the population knew the Allies were advancing toward Paris.

On August 19, the French Resistance called the citizens of Paris to mobilize and join the struggle. By August 20 barricades began to appear all over Paris as the Resistance made ready to sustain a siege. Trees were cut down and trenches were dug in the streets to free paving stones for the barricades. Men, women, and children, using wooden carts transported the materials. Civilians gave their vehicles to be painted and used to transport ammunition and orders to the barricades. Knowing he was losing the battle; Adolf Hitler gave the command to inflict maximum damage to the city and on August 23 German tanks began firing on the barricades. On the night of August 24· the Allies broke into the center of Paris. Hitler had issued orders that Paris must not fall into the enemy's hand unless it was in complete ruins. Despite these orders, German General Dietrich von Choltitz, the military commander of Paris, surrendered to the Allies on August 25 thereby saving the beautiful city from complete destruction. He said later that he realized then that Hitler was insane, and he could not follow the order to destroy such a magnificent city. He described himself as the savior of Paris. While that might be something of an exaggeration, he certainly earned a very special place in history.

That summer new prisoners to Natzweiler brought news of the Allied successes and for the first time many prisoners began to hope they would be liberated. After the fall of Paris, the Allies continued their march through France headed to the German border.

As they advanced toward Germany, the Allies encountered regrouped and entrenched German troops in the Vosges Mountains which resulted in more intense fighting. That mountain range was the last hurdle in the Allied goal of reaching the Rhine. Those mountains were also where Natzweiller was located with its hidden underground factories.

Hitler became maniacal about destroying the remaining European Jews as the Allies marched toward Germany. He ordered the evacuation of Natzweiler before the Allies closed in on it and tried to destroy any records of their dastardly deeds. Orders were issued that under no circumstances were prisoners to fall into enemy hands. Firsthand testimony to the horrors of the camp would be detrimental to the propaganda Hitler was releasing to his people and the world so it had to be covered up. He was moving Jews to the gas chambers of Germany from all over Europe. Historians would later wonder why, when he was fighting a war on two fronts and desperate for fuel, Hitler would use trains and manpower to transport thousands of Jews to concentration camps to inventory them and kill them. His obsession with the destruction of the Jews couldn't be explained. The prisoners from Natzweiler were taken to

Dachau to the gas chambers. Hitler was giving similar orders all over Eastern Europe and Germany. Jews were taken from smaller camps to the main death camps for extermination. His stated goal was the annihilation of all European Jews and time was running out.

Fritz and the prisoners at Natzweiler had no idea that the Allies had liberated most of France or that there was fierce fighting in the mountains surrounding their camp. As the Allies closed in the Nazis became desperate to vacate the camp. On the night of August 31, 140 men were lined up and shot in the neck to start the mass murder of the prisoners. Realizing they couldn't kill them fast enough this way, they began a mass transport to the gas chambers of Dachau. Prisoners in the subcamp system work camps that were situated close to the border in Germany were marched into Germany.

By September 2, the Nazis ordered one block of prisoners after another to stand in formation. They were then marched under heavy guard out of the camp. Day after day prisoners were marched out of the camp with only the clothes on their back, some barefoot. Terrified prisoners worried each day that their block would be the next one called to formation. They had a terrible foreboding they were going to march to their death, and they were right--they were headed for Dachau and the gas chambers. Survivors later called this a death march since they walked through a war zone with bombs and enemy fire all around them and if they survived, they were taken by train to be gassed.

Between September 3 and 4 three trains with 5517 prisoners left the station for Dachau. Natzweiler was the first camp the Allies entered, and it gave them an initial glimpse of the atrocities that had been perpetrated by the Nazis. A surreal scene unfolded as the Allied soldiers approached a completely deserted camp with barbed-wire fences and watch towers encircling it. As hard as the Nazis had tried to destroy all evidence of their evil deeds, many documents still existed and the camp itself bore witness to the conditions the prisoners lived in. Gas chambers and buildings dedicated to human experiments were the first horrific find. Detailed records that had not been destroyed were there complete with pictures, and instruments of torture in plain sight. The gas chambers at Natzweiler were not designed for mass killing but selective murder for the victims subjected to medical experiments. In those records the Allies found records of bizarre experiments with pictures to prove them true. One

Dr. August Hirt had conceived and presided over what was labeled the Jewish Skeleton Project. 59 men and 29 women were chosen as victims due to their perceived stereotypical Jewish characteristics. They were fed well for two full weeks and then gassed. Dr. Joseph Kramer later confessed to personally gassing the victims and shooting one who was fighting for his life. Their skeletons were to be displayed at a University as proof that Jews were an inferior race. Other documented experiments were the intentional murders of inmates with mustard gas, which produced an extremely painful death, infecting them with typhoid, and the use of new gases as they were invented. The only children brought to Natzweiler were there for the sole purpose of testing poisons.

The barracks themselves testified to the conditions the prisoners lived in. They were almost impossible to enter due to the stench. Pictures of the filth and squalor inside would be used to document the conditions the prisoners lived in. The Allied troops were disgusted to think that people lived in a place not even fit for animals. Eventually the barracks were burned to the ground for health reasons.

Dr. Hirt later made a statement that if these were men, he was the most loathsome person. It would seem he maybe had a conscience, but he later said he was justified because they were not human. Dr. August Hirt shot himself before he could be arrested and was later convicted of his crimes posthumously. Dr. Kramer was convicted and hung in the British Tribunal. His confession now hangs in the Natzweiler Museum. Others involved in the experiments were tried and hung at the Nuremberg Doctors' Trials.

The day came when Fritz's cell block was called to formation and marched out of the camp. As they left the gate, military trucks were waiting. The prisoners were loaded onto the trucks like cattle with guards prodding them with machine guns. Each truck was crammed so tight with men they could not move even an arm or leg. Time was running out to evacuate the camp so now the prisoners were transported in military trucks instead of walking to the station. Luckily for Fritz he was one of the last ones loaded and sat close to the entrance of the truck. After the trucks were loaded, the convoy started down the mountains headed for the train station. Of course, the prisoners had no idea they were headed for Strasbourg and the train station. They didn't know that when they reached the station, they would be loaded onto cattle cars like animals and taken to Dachau to the gas chambers. At that point they couldn't move and could barely breathe and could only hope they would soon be off the trucks.

As the convoy made its way down the mountainous roads, it was attacked by the Allies who had no way of knowing that the military trucks contained the very prisoners they were fighting so hard to liberate. The guards hid in the woods leaving their prisoners as sitting ducks for the enemy. Fritz saw the opportunity to escape from their watchful eyes and jumped off the truck and ran as hard as he could. He pleaded with others to join him but only one young man jumped off the truck with him. Knowing he could be shot as he ran, he fully expected to hear the blast of a gun and fall dead as a bullet hit him in his back. Both sides were the enemy to him, the Nazis and the attackers, and one or other could spot him and shoot but he decided to risk it all. Never would he go where the Nazis were taking him; he would rather die. Expecting to hear gunfire or footsteps behind him he ran with all his might. Eventually the sound of gunfire grew more distant and then stopped. As he hid in the forest and tried to catch his breath, he wondered if Nazi soldiers were pursuing him. Did they even know he had jumped off the truck? If so, did they think he was killed in the gunfire. When he caught his breath, he ran hard and fast through the forest. The farther he got, the more hopeful he became that the convoy had left without missing him.

Fritz found a road and walked towards the town of Strasbourg the rest of the day and all through the night until he reached the outskirts of town. When daylight came, he was exhausted and found a place to hide and sleep. Fritz knew the only place he wanted to go was home. All he had thought about for six and a half long years was his family. Thoughts of home and family were what had gotten him through the lonely years of hiding and the cruel years of the concentration camp. All he cared about and all he could think about was finding his family. If the Nazis found him or if a citizen spotted him and turned him in, he faced certain death and Germany was the most dangerous place a Jewish concentration camp escapee could go. Returning to Nuremberg would put him back in the heart of Nazi territory, a place he had escaped six years ago. Even if he died trying, he was determined to find his mother and sister. Nothing else mattered. He planned a careful strategy to hide and sleep during the day and travel at night; he resolutely determined to follow the train tracks and walk to

Nuremberg almost 250 miles away. Considering what his physical condition was, that distance must have seemed like walking to the moon.

Eventually, Fritz found himself walking through farms in the German countryside. The apple orchards were full of fruit that was ripe for the picking. How sweet those apples tasted after years of starvation in the camp. Fritz had only had thin broth with indistinguishable, minute bits of meat floating in it and hard crusts of bread to eat in the camp. Hunger had been his constant companion. Now, he could eat apples until his hunger was satisfied, a sensation he hardly remembered. One night he discovered he could sneak into chicken coops and steal eggs from under the chickens. Now, he had raw eggs and apples to eat and was able to keep his energy up for the long nights of walking. He followed his plan to walk all night long and sleep during the day. The nights were cold by now, but he had been cold for so long he was used to it. By walking all night, he kept himself warm and during the day it was warm enough to sleep. He was afraid to fall into a deep sleep, instead trying to keep alert for any sound, thinking the Nazis might be hunting him down or that a citizen would find him and gladly turn him in. Hopping a train would have been easy and would have expedited his journey but he feared if he was caught, he would have no escape and be shot on the spot. One night he found a bicycle and grabbed it and started riding it. With a bike to ride, he made much better time at night. As he approached his destination, he was surprised that no one saw him or came after him. He fully expected to be shot or arrested at any time. He wasn't afraid though. Every day brought him closer to home and filled him with hope. Finally, he was on the outskirts of Nuremberg.

He waited until it was almost dark his first night there and positioned himself in a hiding spot where he could watch the apartment his aunt lived in. That was the last place he knew that his mother lived. He didn't want to knock too late and startle her, but not too early either as he might be seen. Finally, it was dark, and he went to the door and quietly knocked. As fate would have it, his mother answered the door and as Anna would always tell people, "Just like that, there he was!" One can only imagine the joy they felt as they fell into one another's arms. For Fritz his mother's arms and the warm embrace were a healing balm. He hadn't felt the touch of human kindness for so many years he had forgotten what it felt like. For Anna, this was a miracle. It was as if her son had come back from the dead. Anna held her son and wept for joy. Soon, though, she was filled with sorrow at Fritz's shocking appearance. Like most concentration camp survivors, he was emaciated, and his eyes were sunken and hollow. Anna could feel every bone in his body, and he looked like a walking skeleton. "What had they done to him?" she wondered as she wept. What she didn't realize was that he probably looked better than when he was in the camp after eating all those healthy apples and eggs.

Fritz refused to tell his mother about Natzweiler. Wounds that cannot be seen are more painful and run deeper than wounds that can be seen. He simply could not bear to talk about the camp. The images were horrific: cruel sadistic guards, starvation, filth, disease, rats, lice, hard labor, freezing winters, and death everywhere. The worst part was trying to understand the barbaric, senseless treatment of fellow human beings by the cold-hearted Nazi guards. They took delight in the torture and torment of the prisoners. It was a story of horror that would be unbelievable to most people. Fritz never spoke of what happened in that camp to his mother. He didn't have counselors or support groups to help him cope. He survived emotionally the only way he knew. He simply locked it all away.

Finally, he was home! All that was once taken for granted meant so much to him now, a warm bath, decent food, clean clothes, a clean mattress, a handkerchief; everything was appreciated. There was no "ordinary" in his life ever again. He had only had a quick sink bath with cold water in the camp. Now, for the first time in years, he felt clean. His stomach didn't grumble and ache for food. There were no guards to torment him. He could lay his head on a real pillow and not worry about rats gnawing on his body when he fell asleep. For the first time in more than six years, he could allow himself to fall into a deep, refreshing sleep.

Chapter 10

"The firestorm is incredible, there are calls for help and screams from somewhere but all around is one single inferno."

Margaret Freyer- Dresden survivor February 1945.

Fritz was in hiding again. Worried that the Gestapo would beat his door down at any minute and drag him off, he stayed in the apartment all day. His arrest in France was always on his mind. The fear and terror of that night never left him, and he never wanted to face that again. Prior to his arrest and imprisonment, he had no idea what the Nazis were capable of, but now he had experienced their savagery and vowed that they would not take him alive.

He could not tell his mother how he felt because she wouldn't let him stay in Nuremberg if she knew. Fritz was not going to leave Nuremberg again; he would live there or die there until this nightmare was over.

Being with his mother and aunt was a healing balm. In those precious first days they spent time basking in the miracle of Fritz's homecoming although their joy was always tempered by the fear of the Nazis finding him. As they caught up with each other's stories, Anna realized Fritz could not openly and entirely share what had happened in the camp. Wisely, she did not probe or push, but let him heal at his own pace even though it was hard not knowing what had happened. Just having him home would have to be enough for a while.

Alas, their newly found joy soon turned to grief. Anna's sister brought the devastating news that the Nazis had apprehended Gertrude. Earlier that month a girl at her school had asked the authorities why a Jewish girl was still allowed to be in school. The Nazis soon arrested her and took her to do slave labor in a factory. She was only 16 years old. Fritz was devastated because, of course, he was the only family member who knew firsthand what falling into the hands of the Nazis meant. It seemed they had won after all. How he wished he could rescue her or trade places with her, but the situation seemed hopeless. Memories of the last time he saw her caused his grief to become nearly unbearable. He remembered her as a happy nine-year-old with long beautiful blonde hair and sparking blue eyes, full of life. Hoping she and his mom were safe all this time and dreaming of a happy reunion when this insanity ended, had helped him make it through the darkest days at the camp. He wanted to go to her and comfort her and encourage her to hang on. The Allies would soon rescue them; of that he was certain. Anna was in deep anguish as the news that the Nazis again had one of her family members sank in. It seemed a curse she couldn't escape. First, Arnold, then Fritz, and now Gertrude. For a few days she could relax and enjoy her son and rejoice that he was alive, but with the Nazis on the prowl there was no rest or reprieve. Fritz still could not tell his mother of the cruelty of the Nazis or his fears for his sister which he knew would only compound her grief. How could he help his delicate sister survive? He felt entirely powerless.

His mother and aunt shared what little food they had. Because potatoes were about all they could scrounge up, they had potato soup every day. It was made as creatively as possible with the few ingredients they had but it was a feast to Fritz after the starvation diet he had been fed in the camp. To his dying day, potato soup was one of Fritz's favorite meals. Even after eating it day after day for months, it tasted incredible.

Conditions in Nuremberg were deteriorating fast that fall. Germany was surrounded by the Allies and the enemy was knocking at the gates. The Nazis ordered boys between fourteen and eighteen and men between fifty and sixty into combat. It would be the first time since the days of Napoleon that German soldiers would be forced to defend their own sacred soil. In Nuremberg food and fuel were scarce. The city was almost entirely women and children and they were in a desperate struggle for survival. Gustie's husband was serving the Third Reich on the battlefield. The irony was that Fritz, a Jew, was hidden in a Nazi soldier's house. Anna was fortunate to have a job, but it was agonizing to leave Fritz each day. She worried constantly that someone would find her son and turn him in. What if she came home and he was gone? She couldn't bear it a second time. Soon, though, she and Fritz realized that the people of Nuremberg hardly cared about an escaped Jew in their midst. They were trying so hard to survive that turning anyone into the Nazis was the last thing on their mind. Fritz found he was able to leave the apartment and move around the city freely, helping his neighbors any way he could. Mainly he cut firewood for them and helped scrounge for food. Nobody even questioned why he was there; in fact, they welcomed his help, and many assumed he had been set free. What people didn't know was that you didn't leave a Nazi concentration camp alive; you were worked to death or murdered. If they had been thinking they would have realized that if the Nazis had indeed given Fritz his freedom he would be serving on the front lines.

The Nazis themselves probably didn't know what had happened to him during the raid. Many prisoners were probably killed in the raid when they were left as sitting ducks. Taking time for a body count or identification was out of the question as there was an urgency to get to Germany. For the SS guards it was better the Allies killed off their prisoners since it saved them the trouble.

Air raid sirens started to go off regularly that fall making a haunting, eerie sound as they resonated throughout the city. People ran to underground bomb shelters or basements as fast as they could to wait for the all clear signal. After days of sirens going off and no bombs hitting, people became complacent and started to ignore the warnings. Too many false alarms caused a false sense of security. Because of the Nazi propaganda, most citizens did not realize the Allies were fast approaching their city, or that Germany was starting to collapse. One day the sirens went off and bombs fell on the city. Many people were caught off guard and killed and wounded in the raid. After that people ran for shelter when the sirens went off. That fall there were six major attacks on the city.

By December, conditions in Nuremberg were deplorable. It was one of the coldest winters on record. Coal supplies had been cut off by the Allies and people were starving and freezing. During that time, Gertrude became desperately ill with pneumonia. The Nazis had an old empty insane asylum near Nuremberg where they took the sick from the factories that could no longer work. They were put there on the floor or cots and left to die. Anna found out they had taken Gertrude to the asylum, so Fritz went to take the train to find her and bring her home. He found one train sitting there, abandoned, with the engine blown off. The station was shut down. He went back and got his bicycle and rode it 15 miles to the asylum. There he found his sister barely alive, lying on a cot. Part of the asylum had been bombed while she was lying there. He picked her up and carried her out and not knowing what else to do, he placed her as carefully as he could on the handlebars of the bike and took her home. Anna was able to get her daughter to one of her sister's houses outside of Nuremberg where she hoped Gertrude might receive some medical help. There were no doctors or medical help available, but with her aunt's careful care, Gertrude slowly recovered. Gertrude remembered very little of that time because she was so ill, but she did remember the asylum being bombed and her brother carrying her out and giving her a ride on the handlebars.

On January 2, the air raid sirens went off again. Fritz and Anna were in the main square and ran for shelter under the post office which connected to several buildings; each building had a basement underneath that served as a bomb shelter. Doors connected each basement to the other, so it was possible to crawl through the doors and access any building. The shelter was packed with people. Fritz could never fully explain what happened next. He said he had a powerful urge to start moving to the other end of the basements. He could not ignore it because it was more powerful than anything he had ever felt. Calling to all the people in the shelter to follow him, he opened the first door and started for the next basement. Many, including his mother, followed him, but most stayed put in the first shelter. Fritz opened all the doors with people following him and got to the very end building as fast as he could. After that, bombs started to fall, and all the lights went out. Loud explosions reverberated overhead, and the earth shook. Fritz could hear the building explode above him as the basement rocked and swayed. The explosions kept coming nonstop right on top of them. The noise was deafening. Everyone in the shelter was screaming and terrified. One after another, bombs continued to fall; there seemed to be no end to the onslaught. For the first time Fritz was sure he was going to die. Throughout his long ordeals – hiding, arrest, imprisonment, and escape – he always thought he would survive. But now, as he thought about dying there in a basement bomb shelter after surviving all those incredible odds, he found it particularly sad. The irony did not escape him that the Allies, who were to be his savior, were going to kill him not rescue him. After what seemed like an eternity the all-clear siren went off. As

Fritz and Anna climbed out of the shelter they were greeted by a surreal sight. Their ancient beautiful city was gone. All around them buildings were destroyed, and the city's silhouette was scarred and jagged. Fires were burning everywhere. People were terrified, running and screaming all through the streets. Sirens pierced the air. A gaping hole was all that was left of the post office. All the people who stayed under the post office shelter had perished; only those who had followed Fritz and his mother survived the raid. The Allies had unleashed an unprecedented firestorm of bombs on Nuremberg that day. 1,000 bombers had targeted the city with 1 million incendiary devices and 6,000 high explosive bombs. In that short time, 1,800 people lost their lives, 3,300 were wounded and 100,000 people lost their homes. In a matter of hours ninety percent of Nuremberg was destroyed. The once proud city, home to the famous Nazi rallies, was now reduced to rubble and flames. One witness said that as the people stood and stared in disbelief at what just hours before had been their homes, grief filled the city like a mighty cloak that could not be lifted.

Nuremberg had been chosen because of her symbolic importance as the ideological center of Nazi Germany and because she was Adolph Hitler's favorite city. It was the most devastating attack on a civilian population until the bombing of Dresden six weeks later. The Allies were beginning to employ some of the same techniques that Hitler had used to gain and maintain power; total demoralization of civilian populations. The goals, of course, were liberation rather than enslavement but the results were the same.

Fritz and Anna started to make their way back home. People were walking around stunned, in a state of shock. Everyone was nervous bombs would fall again. The dead and wounded were being carried away on stretchers. In the distance they could hear mournful weeping. It was a hauntingly eerie scene that would burn in their memory forever. It seemed the whole city was on fire. Death and destruction were all around them. Mothers were searching for their children, frantically calling their names. Everybody around them was confused and in shock. Fritz and Anna were relieved to find their apartment building still standing and Gustie alive. With the German press feeding people propaganda that the war was going in Germany's favor, this bombing raid was a shock and wake up call for everyone.

Fritz knew the end was near for Germany. He could only hope Hitler would surrender soon before they froze to death, starved to death, or died in a bombing raid.

By January of 1945, the Russian Army was closing in from the north on Berlin. The American and British forces were approaching the Rhine. The Allies were in the process of a strategic bombing campaign to aid the ground war. Orders had been given for a coordinated air attack called Operation Thunderclap on targeted German cities. The large and intense offensive targeted Berlin and other eastern cities. The Allies hoped the planned attacks would cause confusion and hamper movements of German troops. They also hoped the attacks would have a detrimental effect on German morale and result in a surrender. Berlin, Nuremberg, Dresden, Leipzig, Chemnitz, and Hamburg were all targeted. On February 3, 1945, 1,000 bombers attacked Berlin. In that attack an estimated 25,000 civilians were killed. One of the saddest and most controversial bombings was that of Dresden. Between the 13th and 15th of February, 1,300 heavy bombers dropped more than 3,900 tons of high explosive and incendiary bombs that destroyed 13 square miles of the city and caused a firestorm that consumed the city center. Sadly, the people of Dresden were unprepared, and more than 35,000 civilians were lost. The Allies later defended the operation as the justified bombing of a military and industrial target. Many historians have argued that Dresden was a cultural landmark and the bombing was made to destroy German morale.

Nuremberg was again hit with bombs on February 20 and 21. The Allies were advancing rapidly toward Berlin and clearly winning the war.

For Fritz and Anna, the second bombing raids were again terrifying. The winter was harsh for them with no coal for fuel and very little food. They were constantly on edge waiting for the piercing shrill of the air raid sirens and the distant roar of planes in the air. Nerves were taut and tempers short. There didn't seem to be an end to this absurdity. They were still being fed propaganda that Germany was winning the war. What would it take for Hitler to give up? Would they all be dead first?"

Nuremberg: "It Is Gone."

Chapter 11

"Life does not forgive weakness."

Adolph Hitler 1945

Despite a report to Hitler by Albert Speer on January 30,
1945, stating, "The war is lost," Hitler refused to give in.
It was becoming obvious to his generals that their
Commander in Chief was blinded to reality but the
German armies, at Hitler's insistence, stood and
continued to fight. By February 8, eighty-five divisions of
American soldiers were closing in on the Rhine and by
the end of the month the British and American forces had
reached it. On top of this the Russian army was rapidly
advancing on Berlin. Hitler gave the first indication to his
close followers that he realized he was losing the war on

March 8. From that point on, fear of losing the war took its toll on Hitler's state of mind and his health. Filled with rage, he was continuously screaming and agitated but his fury was now directed at the German people for whom he had previously professed his boundless love. Orders were issued on March 19th that all military, industrial, transportation, and communication installations as well as all stores in Germany must be destroyed. Germany was to be made one big wasteland; nothing was to be left for the people of Germany to rebuild after the war. Hitler revealed in his orders that he had no concern for the post-war fate of the German people. He stated:

"It will be better to destroy these things ourselves because this nation will have proved to be the weaker one and the future will belong solely to the stronger eastern nation. Besides, those who will remain after the battle are only the inferior ones, for the good ones have been killed"

Hitler clearly thought the German people were now the inferior race for losing the war and was not interested in their continued existence. This became known as the "Scorched Earth Order." Due to the rapid advances of the Allied troops, the German people were spared this great catastrophe. Of course, one has to wonder if the German officers who had been entrusted with carrying out Hitler's last commands would actually have implemented a whole scale destruction that would have impoverished their relatives and friends for generations to come. We will, fortunately, never know because they did not have the chance to join in Hitler's suicide plot not only for himself but for the Homeland.

By April, Anna and Fritz didn't know how much longer they could hold out. The living conditions in Nuremberg had deteriorated even more and they, along with the people of the town, had reached a point of desperation. Cold and hungry, people were holed up in their miserable bombed out houses, many dying from hunger and illness. With the infrastructure in Germany destroyed there was no way to get coal or food to the people and shelves were bare. Rumors swirled around town that potatoes were still available in the countryside. With hunger and desperation driving him, Fritz left for the countryside where Gertrude and his aunt were living hoping to find food. Anna could not be persuaded to go; she had become paralyzed with fear from the bombing raids and refused to leave her house. Even though he hated to leave his mother, he had no choice but to go without her and if indeed potatoes did exist there, he would bring some back. This time his reunion with his sister was a joyous one as he was relieved to find Gertrude recovering from her illness and looking much better. Untouched by bombing raids, the countryside's beauty and serenity were a welcome reprieve from the war zone. Best of all they did indeed have potatoes! People were flocking to farmers' homes in the country bringing expensive tapestries and other valuables to trade for bags of potatoes. If he had persuaded his mother to come with him, they could have stayed in this peaceful place away from air raids and bombs until this awful war was over.

Unfortunately, going back to the war zone was the only option he had; Anna was alone in Nuremberg frightened and hungry.

With the Nazi press still announcing a victory for Germany, a bizarre scene was being played out by Goebbels and Hitler in Berlin. Hitler and his closest advisors were hunkered down in an underground bunker in Berlin. From there he was directing the war. Even now, as the Russian Army and Western Allies closed in on Berlin, Hitler stubbornly clung to his hopes of being saved by some miracle. Hitler sent for two horoscopes. One he had had drawn up on the day he took office and one had been composed by an unknown astrologer on November 9. 1918, the day of the Republic's birth. Both horoscopes predicted a reversal of a hard war for Germany by the middle of April 1945. Both predicted Germany would have success followed by a period of peace and rise to power again. This filled Adolf Hitler and Josef Goebbels with a new hope and determination to keep fighting. Fortified by this reading, Goebbels issued a new challenge to the retreating troops. He told them that their Fuhrer had declared a change of fortune would come. Their beloved Fuhrer knew the exact day it would happen, and they would witness a miracle. Despite the fact they were losing the battle and many troops had already surrendered to the Allies, the German Army dug its heels in and continued their hopeless campaign. What would the generals think if they knew their commander-in- chief was directing the war based on astrology charts? What would the German citizens think if they knew their beloved Fuhrer had issued the scorched earth proclamation and wanted to turn Germany into a wasteland? What if they knew their Fuhrer was calling those still alive in Germany inferior and not fit to live because they were losing the war? What if they knew their cowardly Fuhrer was hiding in an underground bunker while the radio was broadcasting that he was on the front lines with his troops?

President Franklin Roosevelt died of natural causes on April 12, 1945. Goebbels heard the news late that night. He convinced himself that this was the turning point for Germany and the miracle they were waiting for. With Berlin in flames from Allied bombings, he ran to telephone Hitler. It was now after midnight and he had the best champagne brought out to celebrate as he congratulated his Fuhrer. It was April 13, the middle of the month, predicted by the stars to be a turning point for them and they were waiting for the promised miracle. Goebbels was ecstatic as he felt Roosevelt's death was a divine judgment, a gift from God. So, it was with Berlin on fire and the enemy closing in that the lunacy in the bunker continued.

On April 16, American troops reached Nuremberg, the city of the great Nazi rallies. As the trucks and tanks rolled into town they were met with a surreal sight; Nuremberg lay in ruins, with piles of rubble everywhere the eye could see, and there was not a person in sight.

Finally, they saw curious eyes peeking at them through curtained windows as they drove through the town. The American soldiers marched to Zeppelin Field, the parade grounds of the mighty Nazi rallies, and in their first order of business hung an American flag over the giant metal swastika towering above the field. In the middle of all the ruin and destruction the American flag proudly waved announcing Hitler was surely defeated. Four days later, a US army combat photographer captured on his movie camera the huge explosion detonated by US troops which destroyed the hated swastika. As this was broadcast in newsreels across America the narrator voiced:

"A swastika will no longer flaunt its crooked arms above the Nazi shrine. The cleansing fires of the war have purged Germany of Nazi power. Let's be sure it never again rises from her ashes."

For the people of Nuremberg, this was a sad and confusing day as they watched in disbelief as American soldiers filled their streets while their radios were still announcing that the Germans would be victors in the war. Now for the first time most citizens realized that they might be losing the war. Desperately they had clung to a thin thread of hope that despite the great odds against them, their beloved Fuhrer would lead them to a miraculous victory. It was, after all, the middle of April and their Fuhrer had promised a supernatural intervention for Germany.

Nuremberg citizens would later realize that they were lucky it was the Americans that reached their city first and not the Russians. The Americans were kind and treated the people with dignity and respect. On the other hand, the Russians gang raped women, and treated the Germans with cruelty and contempt as they rolled into the cities of Eastern Germany. The Soviets considered this payback for the treatment they had received from the Germans since 1941. More than fifty years later when my dad and I were in Nuremberg, we heard repeatedly: "Thank goodness it was the Americans that came and not the Russians." Of course, they were very fortunate they weren't treated as the Germans had treated the people of the lands they conquered.

Fritz and Gertrude had no knowledge of the scene being played out in their hometown. The only information they had was the propaganda from the radio that Germany was certain to win the war. Early the next morning, Gertrude was in the woods walking her aunt's dog when she was startled out of her wits by an American soldier. She was shaking with fear as he approached her and asked questions. Soon her fears subsided as she realized the soldier meant her no harm. Thanks to her continued schooling until she was 16, she was fluent in English. Later that day the American soldiers began searching all the homes in the area and came to search their aunt's home. People were terrified because the Nazis had successfully filled the Germans with fear of the Allies by means of a well-coordinated propaganda blitz. Leaflets had been printed and distributed that warned people of the treatment they would receive at the hands of the Allies complete with graphic descriptions and pictures. They were warned; there would be looting, hunger, deportation, and extermination. Interestingly this description exactly matched the Nazis' treatment of the counties they conquered. Because of the propaganda people were led to believe suicide was the honorable way out, in fact, the only way out, if the Allies succeeded. Because of this many German citizens hoarded cyanide capsules in anticipation of allied occupation. Mass suicides became common in the final days of the war. Life magazine reported:

"In the last days of the war the overwhelming realization of utter defeat was too much for many Germans" Fear of heavy defeat as well as conscience weighed on the Germans. In Berlin alone 7000 committed suicide in 1945 in fear of the dreaded Soviets.

Fritz, though, was overjoyed to see the soldiers. Finally, they were here! For years he had dreamed of the day the Americans would come and rescue him and his family and now here they were before his very eyes. Soon people's fears were eased as the soldiers treated them with compassion and respect. The soldiers were relieved to find Gertrude spoke English. After hearing pieces of their story of survival from the Nazis, the Allies wanted to help them. They offered to take Fritz and Gertrude back to their mother in Nuremburg and help the family in any way they could. Surely, life was about to turn around for Fritz after untold suffering.

As they approached Nuremberg, they were surprised to see Allied vehicles filling the streets and Allied soldiers everywhere. The radios were broadcasting a sure win for the German people. After the soldiers filled them in on the news from outside Germany, they took them to their mother. Now they knew that in a matter of weeks or maybe even days this war would be over. There would be no miracle for the German people. With no more air raid sirens or bombs exploding all around them, Fritz, Anna, and Gertrude could finally relax as they listened to the radio and waited expectantly for the news of Hitler's surrender. Almost seven years before, Fritz had left Nuremberg to escape the Nazis by fleeing to France. Now this saga was ending for him, the Nazis were defeated, and Hitler no longer had the power to harm him.

As the Russians closed in on Berlin, the activities in the bunker became more macabre. Eva Braun had arrived at the bunker on April 15. She had been Hitler's secret mistress for 12 years yet very few even knew of her existence. Now Hitler had called for her to come publicly to his bunker. April 20 was the Fuhrer's birthday. He expressed confidence that day that the Russian army would suffer a bloody defeat in Berlin. His generals were trying to convince him otherwise and urged him to leave Berlin. Many of Hitler's trusted aides were fleeing Berlin as fast as they could. But Hitler would not give up. He ordered a counterattack on the Russians by SS General Felix Steiner. Every available soldier from Berlin was to fight in the attack. Hitler waited anxiously for news of the attack. It was never attempted. It existed only in Hitler's mind and was further evidence of his loss of contact with reality. When he realized on April 22 that the attack had never been attempted, he flew into an intense rage. Witnesses said, "He raged like a madman" and accused everyone of deserting him. The scales were finally falling from his eyes.

On the evening and night of April 28-29 the people in the bunker were ordered to stay awake. Sometime between 1 a.m. and 3 a.m. on April 29 Adolf Hitler married Eva Braun. He had always said that marriage would interfere with his leadership of the people. Now the end of the Reich was near and he was ready to wed Eva. After a brief ceremony in the conference room of the bunker there was a wedding breakfast in Hitler's private apartment. Champagne was brought out and everyone was invited to share in the celebration. Hitler talked on and on (as was his custom) about the successes of his life. He ended the feast with the news that it would be a relief for him to die because his closest supporters and friends had deserted him. Many guests left the room in tears. This wedding would become known as the "death marriage."

Following his wedding, Hitler dictated his last will and testament. In it he still cursed the Jews for all the ills of the world. He also cursed the leaders of his military whom he felt had betrayed him. He ended the lengthy document with a call to the German people to "resist mercilessly the poisoner of all nations, international Jewry." He signed the document at 4:00 a.m. the morning of April 29, his wedding day.

After a situation conference at noon on April 30, Hitler had lunch with two of his secretaries. Eva declined an invitation to join him. After the luncheon, he fetched Eva and together they made a final farewell to his closest followers. Afterward they retired to their private apartment. In a few moments a shot was heard. Upon entering his room those close followers found the body of Hitler on the sofa his face shattered. He had shot himself in the mouth. Eva lay dead at his side. She had swallowed poison. It was 3:30 p.m. on April 30, 1945. With the roar of explosions all around, Hitler was wrapped in a blanket and carried out by his personal valet and an orderly to the garden. Eva was carried out with no covering. They were placed in a shell hole and ignited with gasoline. As the bodies burned, the valet and his assistant retreated to the safety of the bunker while Russian shells rained down on the garden.

There was no public word of Hitler's death; not even the military knew and so his generals continued to fight, even continuing to send him messages. Grand Admiral Karl Doenitz was secretly informed that the Fuhrer had died, and that he had been appointed the Reich President. On the evening of May 1, Josef Goebbels had his personal physician poison his six children, who were happily playing in their private apartment in the bunker, with lethal injections. With their children dead, he and his wife walked around the bunker and bade everyone farewell. Then they went to the garden and at their request an SS orderly shot them in the backs of their heads. There was then a mass exodus from the bunker, and many got through the Russian lines.

Just after 10 p.m. that night radio programs were interrupted in Germany. After a drum roll the announcement came:

"Our Fuhrer, Adolf Hitler, fighting to the last breath against Bolshevism, fell for Germany this afternoon in his operational headquarters in the Reich Chancellery."

Again, the people were fed a boldface lie. Hitler had not died that afternoon but the day before. He had not fallen to the last breath defending his country but had committed suicide holed up in his protected bunker. At 10 p.m. Doenitz himself spoke to the German people and assured them their beloved Fuhrer had died a hero's death. He concluded his broadcast to the German people by assuring them that God would not forsake them.

The Third Reich survived Hitler's death by seven days. On May 7, 1945, Admiral Doenitz radioed his generals that Germany would surrender. At 2:41 a.m. the document of unconditional surrender was signed in a little red schoolhouse in Reims, Germany.

Gunfire and bombs ceased, and the continent of Europe was finally at peace after more than five and a half years of war. After twelve years, one of the darkest ages in the history of mankind had come to an end as the Third Reich dissolved suddenly and completely. While the rest of the world celebrated, it was a dark night for the German people.

Allied Soldiers Enter Nuremberg

German Newspaper proclaiming Hitler died in battle

Chapter 12

"Indifference is the epitome of evil"
Elie Wiesel

As the world woke up to the horrors the Jews had
suffered under the Nazi government, Germany hung her
head in shame. Camp after camp was liberated by the
Allies, and newsreels were shown in theaters everywhere
that contained images from the camps that would haunt
the world. Bodies were stacked like wood in massive
piles ready for the ovens. Survivors looking like walking
skeletons with their bones protruding grotesquely from
emaciated bodies, stared at the cameras, their eyes
sunken, and their expressions blank. Sobering images of
the gas chambers and ovens filled the screen. Soldiers
who liberated the camps would never be the same.

Rounding up German citizens, the soldiers made them walk through the camps to see what had gone on right in their own backyards. Women held handkerchiefs to their noses repulsed by the smells and looked away from the empty stares of the survivors. Could they even grasp the enormity of the suffering? What did they feel as they walked through this cesspool their beloved Fuhrer had created? Shame? Guilt? Repulsion?

In interview after interview with people from the towns there was one recurring theme: "I did not know, nor did I care." Dachau was in the middle of a large city and the smoke from the ovens went day and night. The soldiers said that the stench was the worst they had ever encountered, and they could smell it from miles away, yet the citizens of Dachau chose to ignore it. As people were marched through their towns to train stations and packed on trains like cattle, people ignored them. Hearing the people in the cattle cars crying and begging for help, they looked the other way. Many would walk by the camp every day and could see the people through the barbed wire fence, yet they chose to turn a blind eye to them. Concentration Camp survivor Elie Wiesel, in his book *Night*, stated: "The opposite of love is not hate- it is indifference. Indifference is the epitome of evil."

Every day the news was more horrifying. The sheer number of Jews massacred by the Nazis was inconceivable and for many months it was hard to even guess. The Nazis had destroyed many of the carefully documented records kept at the camps as the Allies approached. People waited anxiously for any word of their loved ones. Little by little a few liberated Jews came home. For most people, however, it was a long, sad wait with nobody coming home. Desperate husbands, wives, and parents posted pictures of their loved ones all over the towns. Did anybody know what happened to them? If they found a survivor from another camp, they showed them the pictures. "Did you see her? Was he in your camp?" For many families the fate of their loved one was not known for years, if at all.

The final number was appalling. Systematically the Nazis had killed more than 10 million people, 6 million of them Jews, a staggering revelation that shocked and stunned the world. For Fritz it was a miracle any had survived, himself included. If Hitler had not been stopped there would not be one European Jew left.

To the American people it was inconceivable that this heinous atrocity had occurred in modern Germany, a country that had given the world so much in art and music, science and education. Germany boasted many of the most respected scientists, composers, and writers in modern history and ironically many of those were Jews. People shook their heads and asked, "How? How did such a thing happen in Germany a civilized country like our own? Why? Why the Jews? Why did the German people allow it?" That humanity would tolerate this kind of evil was inconceivable. To this day, we still ponder these questions frustrated that there is no satisfactory answer. Man's inhumanity to man cannot be comprehended. Books would be written, movies made, and stories told, but the Holocaust could never adequately be explained. Simon Wiesenthal perhaps said it best: "For evil to flourish it only requires good men to do nothing." The Holocaust would be the hallmark of evil and indifference and would always remain one of the darkest chapters in the history of mankind.

Fritz would be tormented for the rest of his life with his own questions as well: "How did the Third Reich rise to such power so quickly? How did Hitler convince the German people to hate the Jews? Why did the German people allow it? Why did they eagerly participate? Why did God allow it? Why did they hate him?" Later in life he would read book after book on the Holocaust trying to find a satisfying answer. For Fritz it wasn't about good men doing nothing or being indifferent. People had actively taken part in his persecution starting with his teachers, neighbors, and peers from the time he was only nine years old. Ordinary people had turned him in to the Nazis in France and a classmate of his sister had turned her in. On every front ordinary German citizens had been vigorously engaged in the verbal and physical abuse of his family. He would always struggle trying to understand the depth of man's depravity during the Holocaust.

The Allied soldiers assured Anna it was safe to return to her home and they were willing to accompany her and her children there. As Fritz, Anna, and Gertrude walked through the remains of their city, the scene struck them as surreal. People were wandering the streets shocked and confused, with men and women openly weeping. They were trying to cope not only with the loss of the Third Reich, but with the utter destruction of their city. The entire city including the once beautiful Pegnitz River was choked with debris. When William Shirer returned to visit the quaint medieval city, he had once covered as a journalist, he said quite simply, "It is gone."

For the most part only the elderly, women, and children were left since fighting age men had been killed, maimed, or taken prisoner in the war. It fell to the women to begin the long arduous process of hauling away the debris. With living space at a premium three to four families were crammed into one apartment and the influx of refugees worsened conditions. Food was scarce and the people were without hope. Everything had suddenly changed, with no more daily propaganda broadcasts on their radios, or loudspeakers blaring, and without any guidance from their Fuhrer they were lost and confused. These very streets had been the scene of the impressive rallies, but now there was not one Nazi soldier to be seen. Nazi flags with giant swastikas were no longer waving in the wind. Swastikas that had been on display everywhere, in store windows, on every classroom wall, on every government building were gone, banned by the Allies who had systematically torn them all down. Blindly and foolishly the people had given their complete devotion to Hitler and now they didn't know what to do or how to act. Seemingly, in an instant their beloved Fuhrer and the Third Reich had passed into history and the German supremacy that Hitler had assured them was theirs had disappeared into thin air leaving them as sheep without a shepherd. All around them their beautiful city and glorious Third Reich lay in ruins and in the rest of the world was looking at them in disgust. Hitler had promised the people a Germany they would not recognize if they elected him and as they looked at their bombed-out city, those ironic words would haunt them. This was indeed a Germany they did not recognize.

Around the world people were celebrating the end of war but not in Germany. Citizens of the countries the Allies had liberated were openly hugging and kissing Allied soldiers. Allied soldiers returning home from the war were met with jubilation. But Germany was in a state of mourning and her soldiers returned in humiliating defeat.

Warily, Anna, Fritz, and Gertrude walked with the soldiers back to their former neighborhood. From a distance they could see that the area had been bombed and as they got closer, they could see their partially destroyed house. Although the entire second story was gone, they were relieved to find the first floor intact and a few rooms still habitable. Surprisingly, some of Anna's beautiful furniture as well as her Rosenthal china had survived both the Nazis and the bombs. Carrying their meager belongings with them, they moved back to the house the Nazis had confiscated nearly five years before. Returning to their neighborhood brought back fears of rejection and torment. Not surprisingly, there was still a strong dislike and distrust of the Jews by the German people. The prejudice of the people did not go away just because the war had ended so anti-Jewish bias did not magically disappear. Jews were still glared at, spit on, and even shot at. Again, the Wolf family was given the cold shoulder by their former neighbors and friends.

Anna and Arnold had not been able to communicate for nearly five long years and it now seemed impossible to contact Arnold with the country in chaos and communication virtually nonexistent. Finally, with the help of the Red Cross, they were able to send Arnold a telegram. One can only imagine his relief and joy when he read the words: "All Alive," Receiving a telegram in return, Anna and her children had a great celebration knowing their beloved husband and father had made it safely to America.

In exchange for Gertrude's help with translating, the American soldiers helped her family any way they could. Eventually the soldiers became good friends with

Gertrude, Fritz, and Anna and their kindness and friendship were a welcome reprieve. They would bring food to the house and Anna would make everyone a delicious home-made dinner and afterward, everyone would play card games and enjoy a relaxing evening together. The stories the soldiers told about their wonderful homeland, the USA, made Fritz and Gertrude more determined to leave as soon as possible. America was the land of promise where they would be safe. Feeling betrayed by his country, Fritz vowed that he would never trust Germany again.

Arnold was able to send packages to his family through the military and those provisions along with help from the Allies kept them alive. Many in Nuremberg were homeless and starving, living in makeshift residences hastily set up in former town halls and museums. Food was scarce and usually available only on the black market. As a result, disease and crime were rampant. Eventually the Allied soldiers were no longer the enemy to the Germans but became, instead, their rescuers.

With the help of the Red Cross and the Allied soldiers Arnold and Anna were able to correspond. After long years of worry and desperation each finally heard the other one's story.

Arnold had barely made it out of Germany alive. Just as he was to be deported, he was whisked away right under the Nazis' eyes. He had false papers that allowed him to travel by train to Italy where a ticket was waiting for him to board a ship bound for America. Arnold was filled with sorrow as he sailed away without his family, leaving them in the hands of the dreaded Nazis. All he could do to console himself was vow to bring them all to the United States as soon as he arrived. Hopefully he was better to them alive in the United States than dead in a Nazi camp. Sadly, his was the last ship to leave Europe with civilians on board due to the escalating war. Later, he learned that bribery kept him from deportation and Anna once again was responsible for the rescue of one of her family members.

Even though Arnold was a stranger to them, Anna's aunt and uncle kindly took him into their home when he reached Salt Lake City. He had arrived penniless with only the clothes on his back. Because he spoke English fluently and had excellent business skills, Arnold was sure he could find a good job. He faced an anti-German bias, however, and no one seemed willing to hire a German immigrant, even a Jew who had escaped Hitler's tyranny. Consequently, this once proud Jewish businessman could only find a job as a taxi driver. With hope that his family would be with him soon, he rented a room in a boarding house and saved every penny he could from his meager salary. By 1941, the world was at war and Arnold, like the rest of the world, had no idea how bleak things were for the Jews in Germany. Hitler by now had issued his "Final Solution" and Jews were being murdered by the thousands every day. With no way to contact his family or hear any news of them, he continued to wait and hope even as the headlines worsened.

As Arnold read and listened on the radio to the devastating events unfolding in Europe it seemed Hitler was unstoppable. France had fallen so fast. Did the Nazis have Fritz? Did they have Gertrude? What about Anna? It was a slow painful realization that he was powerless to get them out of Europe or help them in any way. As he watched the events unfold in Europe one can only imagine the sickening and growing hopelessness of his situation. Returning to his Jewish faith brought him comfort especially through the rituals and prayers at the local synagogue, Other Jews there shared his concern and grief for the Jews in Europe and became a support group for him. Synagogues across the nations were raising money to help the Jews in Europe and pressing the United States to do more. By 1944, the Allied bombings frightened him even more. Even if his family had survived the Nazis how could they possibly survive these bombings? The Allied blitz that destroyed Nuremburg in January appeared in newspaper headlines and newsreels showing Nuremberg destroyed. What if his family was still in Nuremburg? Between Hitler and the Allies there seemed to be no hope left for his family.

After Germany surrendered, Arnold had even less hope that they were alive. News reports were coming in daily with disheartening death tolls of the Jews and civilians in Germany. With Germany in shambles and millions of people displaced or dead, finding his family seemed impossible. Finding transportation to Germany was also impossible and as a result the situation became even more frustrating. So, the news that his wife, son, and daughter had all survived was a miracle. Arnold must have wondered what Fritz and Gertrude looked like. He had last seen Fritz when he was just eleven. That day, seven years before, Anna and Fritz had waved goodbye and left for France. Fritz was only going to work there for the summer. Now he was almost nineteen, a grown man. Gertrude was a little girl of eleven when the Nazis forced them out of their home and took him to the ghetto. She would be nearly seventeen now, a teenager, no longer his little girl. And Anna, his beloved wife. How was she? What did she look like now? Would she still love him? Arnold knew he wanted to bring them all to the United States but what if they didn't want to come? For now, they were safe, and eagerly he made plans to bring them to Utah. Mercifully, he didn't know that it would be nearly two years before they could leave Germany.

Germany had been divided into four zones each occupied by one Allied country, America, Britain, France, and the Soviet Union. The tri-zone of America, France, and Great Britain agreed on several fronts. First was the total denazification of their zones. All Nazi emblems were removed, and swastikas were not allowed anywhere. Any person who had been an active Nazi was not allowed to work in the public sector. All three encouraged their zones to become a democracy and try to halt the spread of communism.

Nuremberg was in the American Zone which turned out to be a godsend to the people. The American soldiers freely shared their food and arranged for The American Red Cross to send CARE packages to the hungry people. Germany had suffered a total collapse of her economy before the war ended. The winter of 1946-47 was the worst people could remember. Coal was still in short supply as well as food and again the people suffered as they did the winter before from cold and hunger. Because of the help of the soldiers and American Red Cross the people began calling America their liberator not their occupier.

Anna, Fritz, and Gertrude fared better than most since Gertrude was working for the Allied soldiers and they had taken their family under their wing. All Fritz and Gertrude wanted was out of Germany. They were filled with bitterness and hatred toward the German people. Anna, on the other hand, thought it would be a good idea to stay in Germany and have Arnold come back. Wisely she saw they owned a home there and Germany was in a good position to rebuild and flourish again and her extended family was there, and she hated to leave them. Arnold, Fritz, and Gertrude, though, were adamant; they would not live there under any circumstances. Germany had betrayed them once and could do it again. All Fritz wanted was to get out of there as fast as he could and never look back.

Anna found a proper lady from England as a tutor for her and Fritz and as a result they were learning very proper English. British accent and all. Their German accent combined with an English accent made it hard for the soldiers to understand them. They were living a life in limbo waiting to hear when they could leave Germany. Ships were busy transporting troops and had no room for civilians. As the days turned into weeks, then months, then years, it became hard to be patient.

In the confusion after the war, Fritz and Anna had the impossible task of finding out the fate of their relatives on Arnold's side. It would take years to sort it all out. Maria, Arnold's mother, was hidden in a convent but died there during the war. Sepp was deported to Dachau and died in the gas chambers. Greta died while in the refugee camp of illness. Ernst's entire family was sent to Auschwitz. There it was believed all of them had perished in the camp. Fritz would find out 50 years after the night he and Ernst were arrested in France that Ernst alone had survived. Hilde, Sepp and Greta's daughter, had her own miraculous story of survival. She and her husband jumped out of the window of a house they were hiding in as the Gestapo were beating down the door. They ran through the forest and escaped the Nazis. My father, brother, and I visited Hilde in France in 1997 when she shared her amazing story of survival. She was widowed by then and her two sons and their families lived in Israel. For Hilde as well as for all Jews, Israel was a dream come true, a truly beautiful thing to rise out of the ashes of the Holocaust. One of our most sobering and poignant moments was when Hilde brought out her engagement picture. There was the entire Wolf family smiling at the camera as they enjoyed the engagement party. Arnold and Anna, Fritz, and Gertrude were there as well as Marie, Ernst, his parents, and little sister. The photo reveals a large group of friends and family gathered to celebrate with Hilde. Hilde looked at the picture and sadly started pointing to people, saying, "Deported, deported, deported." So many in the photo were deported and murdered by the Nazis.

Most heartbreaking was when she pointed to Ernst's beautiful young sister, just a child, and cried as she said, "Deported". To this day I cannot look at that photo without tears forming in my eyes.

Chapter 13

"A thousand years will pass, and the guilt of Germany will not be erased."

Hans Frank 1945

Nuremberg was again cast in the worldwide spotlight when the Nuremberg trials began on November 20, 1945. Following the atrocities carried out by the Nazis, the Allied leaders of Great Britain, the United States, and the Soviet Union issued a joint statement officially acknowledging the mass murder of European Jews and resolving to prosecute those responsible for violence against civilian populations. Since the world had never faced a crisis like the Holocaust there was no precedent for building the framework for an international trial.

Winston Churchill, Britain's Prime Minister, ordered an exhaustive list of criminals to be compiled but did not indicate their specific crimes. He favored executing high ranking Nazi officers without trial. As Anthony Eden explained, "The guilt of such individuals is so black that they fall outside any judicial process." But the Americans and Soviets were not on board with that solution. Not wanting to show the world that democratic states killed without due process the United States felt it necessary to establish a formal proceeding; in addition, there really can be no doubt that summary executions were one Nazi practice they did not want to emulate. Harry Truman, a former lawyer who had succeeded Franklin D. Roosevelt as President of the United States won the Allied powers over and it was decided to establish a military tribunal. The first Nuremberg trail was formally known as the International Military Tribunal and it was there that the very top officials of the Nazi party were tried.

Fritz, like many persecuted by the Nazis, had mixed feelings about the trials. He felt justice could not possibly be served for such heinous crimes and to some extent he was right. In the end they trials were not a big success in punishing Nazi war criminals, but they did set a precedent for international law. The legacy of the trials, and perhaps the most important aspect, was the assembling of public records as proof of the horrific crimes committed by the Nazis. It helped Fritz that the world finally saw what the Nazis were really like and that their brutality could not be denied. For this reason, he became grateful for the trial after his initial misgivings.

Because Nuremberg had been the ceremonial birthplace of the Nazi party it was considered a fitting place to mark the end of the Nazi era. Also, The Palace of Justice in Nuremberg was spacious and largely undamaged by the Allied bombings; and since it already housed a large prison complex security was not nearly as much of a problem as other venues where prisoners would have to be transported on a daily basis from cells to courtroom..

Once again, Fritz saw his hometown become the scene of international intrigue as the international press corps arrived from around the world. This time it was not to report on the impressive rallies and Hitler's rise to power, but to document the Nazis' demise. Now Fritz could wander around town freely and watch the media circus firsthand instead of hiding in his house as he did during the rallies. It was a crazy time in Nuremberg, but he felt satisfaction that the Nazis might be brought to justice. A downside was the continued prejudice on the part of some German citizens against Jews. One wonders about those neighbors who were still treating Fritz and his family with disdain; were they somewhat dismayed to see their former heroes on trial for their lives and their actions now subject to international condemnation?

Wanting to convict the Nazi war criminals with their own words, the American prosecutors felt the best evidence against them was their own records. Even though the Germans had destroyed many of their meticulously detailed records as the Allies approached-- many other records were destroyed in the bombings--the Allied armies had confiscated millions of documents in the conquest of Germany. Allied prosecutors submitted 3,000 tons of records at the trial which were later carefully preserved in the United States National Archives. Further documentation came from the Allied soldiers in the form of still and moving pictures they took of the newly liberated Nazi concentration camps. These images were later transmitted to news agencies that helped to further inform the world about the horror of the camps. As we in the 21st century are painfully aware, some Holocaust doubters still survive though one wonders how they can doubt what is so thoroughly documented. Such denial seems almost pathological.

On November 29, a shocked and silent courtroom watched an hour-long film titled, "The Nazi Concentration Camps." That film was later described as the turning point in the Nuremberg trials because it brought the Holocaust into the courtroom. Also, the Nazis were dedicated to filming graphic images of the atrocities inflicted on the Jews. Photographs and films documented the public humiliation of the Jews, their deportation, mass murder and confinement in the camps. One particularly disturbing picture showed a young woman, naked and about to be shot, begging for her life. Also submitted was the "Stroop Report" which contained pictures that documented the destruction of the Warsaw ghetto. The Allies worked tirelessly to locate, collect, and categorize film records to present at trial; as these were brought forth, the courtroom was stunned and rendered silent by these powerful images It is said that those who live by the sword shall die by the sword; in this case, the Germans were to die at the hands of their own photographs and films.

Eyewitness testimony by the Nazis themselves and by the survivors included details of the Auschwitz death camp, the SS and police units mass murders, and statistics to back the evidence of six million Jews murdered. None of the perpetrators denied the Holocaust or their participation in the atrocities though most tried to deflect their responsibility. "Just following orders" became a kind of litany in the trials.

Key perpetrators openly and frankly gave astonishing evidence related to the Holocaust. Among the most horrifying were testimony from Rudolf Hoess and Otto Ohlendorf. Hoess testified in chilling detail how the gassing of more than one million Jews was accomplished at Auschwitz. In a detached and cold manner, he gave a lengthy summary of his participation in the mass murder of Jews as well as torture and medical experiments. He also testified that the people living in surrounding neighborhoods knew exterminations were taking place at Auschwitz due to the nauseating stench from the burning bodies that permeated the entire area. Hess' testimony was transcribed, and he signed it on April 4, 1946, acknowledging that his statements were true, and his testimony was given voluntarily and not under compulsion.

Otto Ohlendorf testified that his unit, Einsatzgruppe D ,
killed more than 90,000 Jews in southern Ukraine in
1941. Ohlendorf was frank and detached in his testimony
and stated he was just following orders and that he had no
remorse.

Survivors of the Holocaust who directly experienced
Nazi brutalities gave personal and compelling testimonies
of their ordeals that stunned the courtroom and the world.
Marie-Claude Vaillant-Couturier, a survivor of
Auschwitz, told of how she was a seamstress in the camp
and witnessed from the window above her machine the
selection process and people being sent to the gas
chambers. She gave details of the prisoners arriving by
train and being greeted by an orchestra playing happy
tunes as they got off the train. The orchestra was made up
of prisoners forced by the Nazis to participate. As to the
selection process she testified that out of thousands only a
few hundred were spared each time. The others were
taken to the gas chambers disguised as showers. She
watched them strip outside before the eyes of the Nazis
and head for the chamber with a piece of soap and towel
in their hand as they went to their deaths. When the
number of prisoners arriving grew to the point it was hard

for the guards to keep up, they brutally stripped the prisoners themselves and herded them to the chambers.

Walter Cronkite, chief correspondent for the US Press Corps, made this statement while covering the trial: "Those of us who witnessed the Nuremberg trials, as well as those who organized and participated in them, were highly conscious of the fact that history was being made." Prosecutor Benjamin Ferencz later said that it was as if he had peered into hell, and that the "defendants' faces were blank all the time, absolutely blank. It was as though they were waiting for a bus." George Sakheim, an English translator for the trials, wrote that nothing could have prepared him for what he would encounter in Nuremberg and that the recounting of the atrocities was sometimes so horrible and gruesome that it surpassed anything the human mind could imagine. Chief United States prosecutor Robert H. Jackson called the defendants arrogant and contemptuous.

Of the 24 tried at the first tribunal hearing 18 were found guilty; of those, 11 were sentenced to death, one in absentia, and four received sentences of 10 years to life. Rudolf Hess, fittingly, was hanged at Auschwitz.

For survivors like Fritz and most who were involved or followed the trial this seemed an inadequate punishment considering the enormity of the crimes. Many wondered if there was any use in having the trials at all as nothing would bring back the lives of 6 million people. So many of the perpetrators had fled or not been charged which angered many who considered the trials too small in their scope and incomplete. Even the 12 subsequent trials seemed inadequate to the masses. Despite this, the Nuremberg trials left a legacy in the world. The trials established that all of humanity deserved to be guarded by a legal shield and even a head of state could be held criminally responsible for crimes against humanity. The creation of the International Military Tribunal after the trials has served as a model for other tribunals; the trials have influenced international criminal law and served as models for other conventions dealing with genocide.

For the victims, the trials validated their experiences and documented the horrors of the Holocaust. After this no one could honestly deny what had happened or minimize the enormity of the Holocaust or the sheer lunacy and brutality of the Nazis.

Hans Frank, the notoriously brutal Governor General of Nazi occupied Poland, was tried and found guilty during the Nuremberg trials. He perhaps summed up what the world was feeling before he was hanged: "A thousand years will pass, and the guilt of Germany will not be erased."

Perhaps the most disturbing of the tribunals was the Doctors' Trial which began on December 9, 1946. Twenty-three medical doctors were tried on charges of mass murder under the guise of euthanasia and human experimentation. Josef Mengele, one of the leading doctors, had evaded capture. More than 1500 documents with photos were assembled for the trial and 85 witnesses testified including the doctors and the victims themselves. Medical experiments had been conducted on thousands of prisoners with the majority dying from procedures. Those who survived were generally left permanently crippled, mutilated, or with weakened bodies and mental distress. From records the Nazis themselves kept and pictures and detailed accounts, participants in the trial saw limbs being hacked off living inmates with no anesthesia, inmates left in tanks of ice-cold water to see how long it took them to die, and inmates deprived of oxygen to see how long they would survive. Bone, muscle, and nerve tissues were taken from victims without anesthesia causing great agony and mutilation with their ordeals filmed and preserved. Inmates were given mustard gas, various poisons, and injected with malaria and jaundice. Most disturbing were pictures of children being tortured until they died. The experiments were cruel, tortuous, and inhumane.

Joseph Mengele, who continued to escape capture and ultimately died of drowning in South America many years later, was one of the most notorious doctors in Auschwitz; he was tried in absentia. His experiments on twins brought to the camp were repulsive and shocking. At his request contemporaneous pictures had been taken of his victims and the experiments. One picture presented in the courtroom showed four emaciated boys (2 sets of twins) staring blankly at the camera. Out of 1500 sets of twins, only 200 survived his brutal experiments. As pictures and records of the human experiments were presented in the courtroom, reporters and witnesses openly wept. More shocking evidence came as the doctors on trial and the victims themselves testified. Vivien Spetz, a reporter covering the trial, said she could no longer watch, but had to put her head down and weep. She said the photos from the trial were seared into her

memory and would never leave her. The victims'
testimonies were personal and powerful with many
showing scars and mutilations on their bodies. One
testified without a voice because his vocal cords had been
destroyed by the experiments. Many of the accused
doctors gave dispassionate accounts of brutal and sadistic
acts performed on their victims.

This was the first time Fritz heard of the appalling
medical experiments performed in his camp. The doctors
on trial from his camp openly confessed to the
experiments on victims which included infecting them
with typhus and subjecting them to mustard gas and
phosphene gas. Dr August Hirt who ordered 86 inmates
gassed at Natzweiler so their bones could be studied had
committed suicide but was still tried in absentia. His
carefully documented records of the experiment and
photos were presented as evidence. Dr. Josef Kramer
personally gassed the victims for the experiment and
confessed that he observed through an exterior opening
his victims dying in the gas chamber and concluded, " I
felt no emotion when preforming these acts."

Finding out that these atrocities happened in his own
camp caused Fritz much anguish and he wondered if any

of his comrades singled out and taken by the Nazis had suffered similar fates. Already he was suffering from survivors' guilt and the experiences associated with the trials compounded it immensely.

Of the 23 doctors tried, 16 were found guilty and 7 were sentenced to death and again this seemed a miscarriage of justice considering the scope and nature of the crimes. But good came from this trial as well as The Nuremberg Code was established giving clear rules about what was legal and what was not when conducting human experimentation. Also, the assembly and documentation of the records of the Doctors' Trial again gave the world proof of the atrocities committed by the Nazis.

The Nuremberg trials with their massive press coverage brought the Holocaust into people's homes all over the world. Images were seared into their memories that were shocking and repulsive. Germany's press had been particularly quiet with very little coverage of the trials. Many Germans were eager to forget or claim ignorance of the crimes. Prosecutors wanted the world to know that most German people were aware of the Nazis' cruel treatment of the Jews and chose to actively participate or ignore the situation altogether. Essentially, the Nuremberg trials established irrefutable evidence of the Holocaust with not only the intent to bring justice but prevent this from ever happening again. Chief American prosecutor Robert Houghwout Jackson summed it up perfectly: "The wrongs which we seek to condemn and punish have been so calculated, so malignant and so devastating, that civilization cannot tolerate their being ignored, because it cannot survive their being repeated." Fritz felt that if the trials stopped another Holocaust from ever happening again, they did indeed succeed.

The Nazis own photos were used against them in the trials

Map titled: "Executions carried out by Einsutzgruppen A"

Nazis took pictures of their victims before and after they were shot

Here the women are forced to take off their outer clothes before the picture is taken

Selection process coming off train

Nazis labeled this photo below Crematorium 1 and 2

Unsuspecting women and children were headed to their death

The Ovens

The pictures presented at the trials from the liberation of the camps shocked the world

Gold rings taken from victims

Evidence collected and documented
for trials

Chapter 14

"This Above All Else"

The Salt Lake Tribune

Fritz was frustrated with the waiting time to leave Germany. He assumed they would be allowed to leave as soon as the war ended, and he was ready! By May of 1946, one year later, there were still no ships transporting passengers out of Europe. His family was living in a state of limbo in their bombed-out house. Making plans of any kind was impossible knowing they could get notice at any time that a ship was ready. To keep busy and pass the time, Fritz helped with the seemingly endless cleanup of debris and worked on his English. Gertrude continued to translate for the Allied soldiers.

The Allied soldiers occupying Nuremberg had faced a daunting task after the war. With the complete collapse of

the Nazi government the Allies had to form a system of
government and control with infrastructure to match.
Tensions ran high the first year since the Allies and
Germans had very recently been bitter enemies and had
very little trust for each other. Many Germans were
reluctant to let go of the Nazi ideals and their hatred of
the Jews made it even harder for the Allies to keep the
peace. On the other side of the coin, the Allied soldiers
wanted to go home and resented having to stay in Europe
for the sole purpose of policing the German people.
Almost miraculously, tensions eased pretty much without
warning or reason just before the summer of 1946 and the
Germans and Americans became comfortable with each
other even forming friendships. One theory is the German
children broke this barrier of distrust since they were
curious about the Allied soldiers and not afraid to talk to
them and become their friends. Also, by 1946, Western
Germany's economy had started to improve and the
people finally had a sense of optimism for their country.
America, France, and Great Britain occupied separate
sections of Western Germany with the Soviet Union
occupying Eastern Germany. Eventually all of Western
Germany was unified, and the goal of the Allies became
to help her form an independent government that could

rebuild from the war. This new spirit of trust and cooperation made it possible in one decade to transform Western Germany from a Nazi totalitarian government to a democratic nation with an economy that was thriving. In 1948 the United States gave 12 billion dollars in economic assistance under the Marshall plan to help rebuild Western European spirits and economies. Due to the dramatic transformation of the country, the Allied occupation of Germany was considered one of the greatest successes of American foreign policy in history.

Western Germany was flooded with people trying to leave Europe, making it almost impossible for ordinary citizens like Fritz and his family. Adding to the bottle neck, Allied soldiers needed transport ships to return home, and thousands of displaced persons from the concentration camps and other countries were desperately trying to leave Germany and were, quite logically, given priority. By 1946 little had seemed to change and the drudgery of day to day living continued.

But finally, the long-awaited day arrived. Anna, Fritz, and Gertrude were scheduled to leave on a troop transport ship, the SS Marine Flasher, on February 27, 1947. In the summer of 1946, the ship was commissioned to bring Holocaust survivors and displaced persons from Germany to America. The waiting list was long for those waiting for transport and it seemed forever until it was their turn. For Fritz and Gertrude this was a time of celebration. They both wanted out of Germany as quickly as possible. Anna, on the other hand, was torn. Seeing that Germany was making a good recovery, Anna saw some benefits to staying; after all, she reasoned, they owned a home and could rebuild their lives and ask Arnold to come back to them. Besides, her close extended family was in Germany, she was nearly 50, and a move across the ocean to a new country and culture would be hard on her. Her family, though, would have nothing to do with staying in Germany. Arnold, Fritz, and Gertrude despised their homeland and swore they would never trust Germany again. Fritz and Gertrude would leave with or without their mother and never look back.

Packing the few belongings they were allowed to take on the ship they prepared to leave. Anna gave her beautiful furniture, china, and household goods to her relatives. For Fritz the hardest thing to leave behind was his beloved train set. Somehow it had survived the Nazi occupation of their home and he sold it to help pay for the trip. Anna closed the door on the first and only house she would ever own and walked away with her children.

Once again, Fritz was at the train station to leave Nuremberg. This time he hoped never to return. Someday the better memories from his childhood would return and he would reminisce nostalgically about the train station. But at this time, the station still symbolized all the sorrow of his life. He rode the train with his family to the port of Bremen where the ship was waiting, and he never looked back.

It was a bit of a shock to see the ship they would be on for eleven days; it was a basic troop transfer ship with no luxuries at all, not even beds. Hammocks hung along the walls where men and women were divided for sleeping. Fritz didn't care. At last he was leaving Germany and by this time he was willing to swim to America to get out of there. As the ship pulled out of the harbor Fritz turned his back to Germany refusing to even look as his native country disappeared over the horizon. He was leaving with a bitter heart and hatred of the Nazis and if he could somehow extract revenge he would. If he could somehow go back to his former classmates and teachers and make them feel his pain and shame, then he would. Those horrible boys from Hitler Youth were probably dead by now, killed in the war, but he would gladly beat any that survived. The SS guards and prison guards deserved to die. And what about God? Where was He? How could He let this happen? Finally, he decided there could not be a God because if there was one the Holocaust couldn't have happened. Later in his life when he could not live with the pain and bitterness any longer, God would gently reach out to him and draw him near and Fritz, through God's power, would forgive the Nazis and be healed. But it was a long way from that sea going adventure to a new life.

The voyage turned out to be a rough one on the turbulent winter ocean waters. Almost all the passengers spent the entire time seasick and vomiting. Anna and Gertrude stayed below in their hammocks too sick to get up. Fritz found he felt better on the deck away from the stale and putrid air below. He spent most of the voyage on deck enjoying the company of the deck hands. One passenger did not survive the passage and it was a somber moment as the entire ship observed the burial at sea.

As the ship churned into the New York Harbor aided by tugboats, every single person was on deck cheering and clapping. Hundreds of people were at the harbor to welcome the weary travelers to America. Most of the passengers were Jewish Holocaust survivors. Many New York Jews routinely came to the harbor to welcome the SS Marine Flasher every time she arrived back in New York. They were paying their respects to their fellow Jewish brothers and sisters, remembering the tremendous suffering they had endured as well as rejoicing in their safe arrival on American soil. It was a time of celebration.

The American Red Cross was there to aid the travelers with food and clothing. They helped transport Fritz and his family to the train station to start the cross-country trip to Utah. Surprisingly they found they had a Pullman car with beds for their comfort and after their rough sea voyage, the train ride across the United States was pure luxury. All of them were eager to see Arnold and their new home.

As the train rolled into Utah, Fritz was mesmerized by the beauty of the area. The snow-capped Wasatch Mountains towered over Salt Lake City and the air was crystal clear. In many ways they reminded him of the beautiful Bavarian Alps in Germany.

As they stepped off the train Arnold was waiting, overcome with emotion. One can only imagine his thoughts and emotions as he watched his family emerge from the train. Reporters from the *Salt Lake Tribune* were on hand to capture the story. The title and picture that appeared in the paper, "This Above All Else," summed up the years of suffering and, now, the tears of joy. As Arnold wrapped his family in his arms, he knew God had granted a miracle. After fleeing Germany seven long years ago he was finally re-united with his beloved wife and children.

While this part of the story ends here, the saga continues until the present day. For new generations have replaced the older ones, the way of life. New hope has replaced older despair and family celebrations have replaced family grieving. The work of this author may be complete with these words, but new authors will surely replace her and add to the story of a truly remarkable family that survived because of strength of will. May the peace of God which passes all understanding fill your hearts and minds.

r Cloud Has Silver Lining

The Salt Lake Tribune was on hand to capture their miraculous reunion

...other again—this time in another country—is the Arnold Wolf family, longtime residents of Nuernberg, Germany. Gertrude, left, Mrs. Wolf, ...

Mr. Wolf and Fritz, whose reunion ended a separation of seven years, during which time Mr. Wolf has lived in Salt Lake City, smile after war years.

Utahns Sought For Jobs in Merit System

THIS ABOVE ALL!

German Family Reunited In S. L. After 7 Years

THIS ABOVE ALL!

German Family Reunited In S. L. After 7 Years

Bewildered as to what names they should have in America—and wanting above all else to be Americans—the Arnold Wolf family from Nuernberg, Germany, subjected during the war to typical "treatment of Jews" under the nazi regime, Friday arrived in Salt Lake City.

The long another trip across the Atlantic and the long train trip from New York to Ogden reunited Mrs. Wolf, Gertrude, 18, and Fritz, 20, with husband and father Arnold Wolf, after a separation of seven years.

Mrs. Wolf wasn't sure just what the American version of her name should be—Annie or Anna—but after an involved conversation in German she decided on the former spelling. Fritz, similarly, thinks

he should be "Fred" in America, and may adopt the Americanized spelling.

Feeling nothing but relief and happiness over leaving Germany, their home until now, the mother and two young people "adopted" Salt Lake City immediately.

Speaking in broken but sincere English, they described in wonder their impressions of the Wasatch range capped with snow and the warm sunlight shining upon homes and yards not devastated by war.

Mr. Wolf left Nuernberg seven years ago and came to Salt Lake City almost at once. He has been a citizen of the United States for more than a year, a goal his family is eager to achieve. Because he is Jewish, Mr. Wolf left Germany before the war, and his children —although they are not fully Jewish—were subjected to "treatment" by the nazis.

Content to just sit back and relax for awhile, and not wanting to "talk about" Germany during the war, when Fritz was confined to a concentration camp and Gertrude was forced to do factory work when she was 16, the two young people are undecided about their immediate futures. They want to work, and they want to continue with their educations. But most of all the family wants a place—some place—to live. Presently they're all staying at the boarding house at 387-1st ave. where Mr. Wolf has lived since coming to Salt Lake City.

Epilogue

The wound left by the Holocaust was an almost
unbearable burden for my father for most of his life. Even
though we never talked about his story in our home, like
so many children of survivors I grew up in the shadow of
the Holocaust. I did not realize until adulthood that my
father's experiences in Nazi Germany had to some degree
shaped my life, too. During my growing up years the
facts of Nazi concentration camps were treated as a dark
family secret. Even though we were not allowed to ask
questions or mention it, it still permeated every aspect of
our home and hovered over us like a dark cloud. At
times little tidbits would escape as my parents talked in
hushed voices not knowing I was listening. But if I asked
questions I was scolded with, "Don't bring your father
pain" or some expression much like that. Since I never
wanted to hurt him, I learned to keep questions to myself.
When I was very young, I heard my parents say "Nazis"
and "concentration camp." At that age, I had no idea what

those words meant or why hearing them brought such pain to my father. The hurt was physical and visible, like someone had punched him in the stomach.

In my confusion I thought perhaps my father had done something horribly wrong, something to be ashamed of. Since that scared me, I learned to leave the room when they began to whisper or lower their voices. Since I was a sensitive girl with a propensity to worry, the sense of isolation which I came later to know I shared with my father and mother were nearly overwhelming. I have learned through study, conversation, and listening that my reactions are very common in the families of survivors of traumatic experiences. But, of course, I did not know that as a small girl.

To the outside world, we were a typical suburban family in the 1950's and 60's. My father, Fred, nee Fritz, Wolf, worked at Sears and my mother, Dorothy, was a typical and very good homemaker, as we used to call moms who stayed home. My father left for work every morning at 8:30 a.m. and was home by 6:30 sharp. When his car pulled in the driveway, I would run to him to be swept up in his arms. The rhythm of our life was comforting, and it was a safe and comfortable place to be.

Many times, he brought me surprises from the store, fun little toys or other goodies. One day he showed up with two tiny kittens. My mother was as astonished as I was but not as thrilled. My mother's week was ordered by a strict schedule--laundry on Monday, errands on Wednesday, baking on Thursday, ironing on Friday, and cleaning on Saturday. Sunday was a day for church and a pot roast dinner. My father was a quiet man. I do not recall a time that he raised his voice to me. He was always loving and kind to his family and friends and had an inner strength that I could feel when he hugged me, or when I sat on his lap. He was usually happy and outgoing and loved to talk to anyone who would listen. After I learned his story, I realized how much strength it took for him to be that way. Thin and athletic, he seemed strong to me and I had lots of experiences by which to judge since he and I did a lot together by ourselves. He took me sledding in the winter and swimming in the summer creating wonderful memories for me.

But he had periods of deep melancholy. He would become inexplicably sad and want to be left alone. As frightening as this was for me, we never discussed it. My strong father, my hero, appeared fragile during those episodes. They were not frequent but when they occurred, they shook me to the core. He was so sad and lost. The quiet, gentle father that I adored was in pain and I could do nothing to help him; he wasn't invincible. Much older and maybe a bit wiser I now realize the infrequency of these periods was a sign of great strength in him rather than weakness. But back then it was different. I had this irrational fear that my father was dying. Sometimes I would start crying right in the middle of a family activity for no apparent reason. I tried to explain to my mother when she asked, "Why on earth are you crying?" I started once to tell her about my worry, but she dismissed it and told me not to be so dramatic, that nothing was going to happen to my father.

Many times, he would bury himself in his library of books on the Nazis and the Holocaust. "The Rise and Fall of the Third Reich" (with black tape covering the swastika on the cover) was dog-eared. He read it over and over searching for answers. Why did the Nazis hate the Jews? Why did they hate him? How could they have risen to power? How could Germany allow the Holocaust? The question that seemed to trouble him the most was how the human heart could become so dark. He was searching, of course, for answers to age old questions that no one can give. Until I was older, it was a mystery to me what these books meant and why he read them over and over. I even wondered why he had covered the swastika.

Often, he would retreat to the backyard to listen to music. His classical albums and record player were among his prized possessions and Beethoven was his hero. He would go to the back patio and set the record player up, get comfortable, sit back and become absorbed in the music. When I joined him, I enjoyed the music and the comfort of sitting with him. I am forever grateful to him for passing along his appreciation for classical music. As he listened, tears would stream down his face. I was not scared because his face was serene, and the pain was gone.

I didn't know then that listening to the majestic music of Beethoven was part of his healing and his path to God. Years later he told me that music played a part in his journey to faith; there had to be a God though he had resisted His love for many years because nothing that beautiful could come from man. He also said that the love of his wife and children and the beauty of the world around him brought him to a place he could begin to seek God and not deny His existence anymore. He left

Germany an angry and bitter man. He hated the Nazis
and Germany. He did not want to believe in God because
he couldn't reconcile a loving God with the Holocaust.
But hate and bitterness took such a toll on him that he
couldn't heal and be whole, not while harboring such
angst.

I was probably 11 years old when I first read "The
Diary of Anne Frank" which explained the Holocaust to
me through a young girl's eyes in terms I could
understand. It took a while for me to connect her
experience to my father and realize that was what my
father had endured. For some reason, maybe to protect
him in retrospect, I wanted to deny he had suffered like
she had. It was hard to process because there was no one
to talk to about it. I finally realized it wasn't shame that
kept my father quiet, but pain. After that realization I
started to wear his experience like a badge of courage.
"My father is a Holocaust survivor" I would proudly
proclaim. But that created another problem; people would
ask questions I could not answer like, "What camp was
he in?" or, "How did he survive?" I had no answers. I
knew only that he had survived a Nazi concentration
camp which was hell for him. None of my friends
believed me. I wanted answers but didn't know where to

turn. By high school I was reading all the books I could get my hands on that were written by Holocaust survivors. This helped somewhat because even though I didn't know my father's personal story, reading about others made me understand him better. Or so I thought, anyway, and that gave me a certain amount of peace.

When asked what he did in Germany my father's standard reply was, "I worked in an airplane factory." To some degree that was true since he did work in an underground airplane parts factory in the camp. And when he was deported as a boy, he was told he was going to work in a factory. The Nazis had a way of keeping the deportees from panicking. This was one: "We have a job for you. You must report." People did not realize that a healthy teenaged boy during World War ll in Germany would either be conscripted into the Nazi army or deported to a camp. There was no in between. My father simply did not want people to know his history which I came to understand much later in life. Sometimes people thought I was making the whole camp thing up. Finally, like my father, I came to a point when I did not talk about it. I had lived a long time with the hidden mystery of my father's past and finally came to a place of acceptance that I would never know what had happened. If there are family members of Holocaust survivors reading this, they will know the feeling, I am sure.

There came a time when my father came home from work in the middle of the day and crawled into bed. He refused to come out. He didn't leave his bedroom for days. No one explained things to me, but our house was constantly full of people trying to help. His co-workers came, his sister, his friends, finally even our pastor. Everybody was worried. This struggle, though, was between my father and God and my father had to face it alone. Finally, he refused to see anyone. I was terrified since I had never seen him like this. All I was told was that it was work related. To my knowledge then and now, only my mother knew the reason for his sudden depression and seclusion. It was another shadowy secret that our family tiptoed around.

I wasn't even allowed in his room. I was afraid he was dying and perhaps in a way he was. He was dying to the pain he had carried for so many years, mourning the life the Nazis had stolen from him, and embracing a new life, one that God had for him. Out of this brokenness a beautiful new man would emerge. I think he had reached a point where the pain was unbearable. He was at a crossroads where he could choose to forgive the Nazis or let them control his life forever.

He chose the path of forgiving his persecutors in the quiet chamber of his bedroom and embracing God's love. He was a changed man after that never again to be chained by anger and bitterness. God brought beauty out of the ashes of the Holocaust. The Nazis had taken away his education, self-esteem, and confident spirit and much of that could never change. But with the help of God, he was at last able to let go of what might have been and accept the new plan God had for his life, a different plan but even more beautiful. I didn't know until years later what happened in that bedroom. I just knew that after he finally emerged from the room things were different. Even at my young age I knew that finally my father was at peace.

I could have extended him a lot more grace instead of ingratitude had I known his story sooner. But it took many years for me to comprehend how his experiences had affected him and what a miracle it was that he could be a loving father and I could have a happy, normal childhood. World War II had ended just six years prior to my birth and the hurt and pain still had to be fresh and raw. Many children of Holocaust survivors do not have this sort of experience to lean upon. I have heard and read many stories of survivors who buried their pain in alcohol, drugs and other forms of escape from life. Many were angry and took it out on their families with verbal or physical abuse. Depression was a huge problem. Back then, there were no counselors or support groups for the victims. They had survived unimaginable abuse and were certainly suffering from post-traumatic stress and worse. Without God's help I don't see how any survivor could become whole and well. The well-documented atrocities inflicted on the Jews are these days beyond our comprehension; the wounds were deep and painful. Without healing they fester, grow and bring death whether physical, spiritual, emotional, or psychological. A person simply cannot bury such pain. It will surface. I'm grateful that I finally did hear my father's story. His story is not only of suffering and pain, but also of forgiveness and wholeness. Hearing his story made me love and respect him more. He is and always will be my hero.

I would like to thank my husband, Clyde, for all his help and patience during the long process of writing this book. Also, my daughter, Rachel who encouraged me and helped with ideas for the story. My family was so patient, and I am grateful for their support. I want to give a special thank you to my editor, Tim Hunt. He endured many frustrating months with me and never gave up. The United States Holocaust Memorial Museum helped with my research and provided my father's arrest documents Their efforts to help find documentation for family members of Holocaust victims is invaluable and greatly appreciated.

Made in the USA
Coppell, TX
09 April 2021

53375540R00152